Tomorrow

First Edition

Published by the Nazca Plains Corporation
Las Vegas, Nevada
2015

ISBN: 978-1-61098-310-5
E-Book: 978-1-61098-311-2

Published by:

The Nazca Plains Corporation®
Austin TX 78755

PUBLISHER'S NOTE

Tomorrow is a work of fiction created wholly by Lew Bull's imagination. All characters are fictional and any resemblance to any persons living or deceased is purely by accident. No portion of this book reflects any real person or events.

Getty Images (US), Inc.
Art Director, Kimm Antell

To Derek,
Thank you for your great advice and delightful
sense of humor shown throughout the writing of this book.
It's greatly appreciated.

Tomorrow

First Edition

Lew Bull

Contents

CHAPTER 1

If a bird were to fly over the luxurious house at 18 Ravenswood Place, it would have seen a refreshing swimming pool with two men lying on pool loungers sunning themselves. The older of the two men, Fred, is the owner of the house and next to him is his son, Peter.

Peter glanced across to his dozing father and smiled. He admired his father, for not only the way in which he had brought him up once his mother had divorced Fred, but he also admired the way his father had taken the trouble to take care of his body. He looked at Fred's smooth buffed chest, over the flat stomach to the bulge, encased in the bright canary yellow Speedo, down to the thick muscular legs and finally to the feet.

"Hey Dad, you know what they say about guys with big feet?"

Fred never moved when he heard the question. Without opening his eyes, he asked, "What?"

"I said did you know what they say about men with big feet?" repeated Peter.

"I heard you the first time, but what's the point and who are they that you're referring to?"

"People say things about men with large feet."

Fred opened his eyes and turned to face Peter.

He smiled and said, "Have a look at the size of your feet Peter. I think you inherited them from me."

Peter instinctively looked at his feet and saw that they were just as large as his father's and smiled.

"Does that answer your question, son?"

"I suppose so," blushed Peter, adjusting the lie of his cock and balls in his pale blue Speedo.

"Now are you coming in for a swim?" enquired Fred, rising from his lounger and diving into the cool, clear water and surfacing at the other end of the swimming pool.

Peter did not hesitate and was soon surfacing from the water next to his father.

"Dad, I remember you telling me about the firefighter that you used to visit, many years back; was he the reason that Mum divorced you?"

"I don't know if I would say that he was the reason, son, but it was because of my sexuality that she divorced me. When she found out I was gay, that was when things started to go downhill so to speak. I must say, though, our parting was amicable and there haven't been any ill feelings between your mum and me."

"I know you still love her," replied Peter.

"Of course I do, but it's a different type of love now."

"But are you happy, Dad?"

"Absolutely! Living here and having my friends to visit, what more could I ask for? The only thing that I think I need to do is find myself some part-time work to do, as I'm beginning to get a little bored some days."

"Have you thought of anything in particular, Dad?"

"No, not really son, but I'm sure that something will come along."

"Have you ever heard from Patrick, my old sports coach, after he left you, Dad?"

Fred smiled as he thought back to his first meeting with Patrick.

It was when Peter and a group of his friends, including his sports coach Patrick, had arrived for a weekend. Fred had recently been divorced so having the younger company in his house was a break from the mundane loneliness. It was during this weekend that he and Patrick realised that they had much in common and this led to them sharing Fred's bed for the weekend and getting to know each other better. They had continued to see each other for months after the first visit. In fact, they had a relationship that lasted about eight months, then Patrick transferred to another college, and this meant that the visits became fewer until both men drifted apart.

"Do you miss him, Dad?"

Fred smiled at the thought.

"Of course I miss him. He was good for me and he filled a void in my life."

"Have you thought of finding someone to take his place?" asked Peter.

Fred roared with laughter.

"You make it sound like a boyfriend is just something to replace, much like a broken object. Just because you lose one doesn't mean you have to immediately replace him."

Fred swam back to the other side of the swimming pool to where the loungers were and climbed out of the water, his Speedo clinging to his taut body and water dripping from him as he walked. He lay down on the lounger again and let the sun begin to warm his body once more.

"Any chance of a drink?" enquired Fred, stretching his body and then relaxing.

"What would you like, Dad?"

"How about us each having a martini?"

Peter swam to the side of the pool nearest to the loungers and he too climbed out, dripping water onto the concrete path around the edge of the pool. Fred lay there looking up at his son. He smiled at him, admiring the trim, slim body and feeling proud that his son had grown into a fine young man.

Peter ran into the house and started making the martinis. In a flash, he was back at the pool, handing Fred his drink and then lying down on his lounger, drink in hand.

"Cheers, Dad."

"Cheers, son. Here's to us!"

They both took a sip of their drink and placed their glasses on the small tables adjacent to each pool lounger.

"How are things with you and Keith?" asked Fred.

"Fine, Dad, just fine."

"So where's he today? Why didn't he come with you?"

"He's busy, Dad. He's got a photo shoot with a model today so I thought I would leave him to it and come on my own."

"Oh," replied Fred, a little distantly.

"What happens at these photo shoots?"

There was a moment's pause and then Fred asked another question.

"How do you mean?"

"Well, where do they have them and what are they for?"

"Oh, sometimes they have them outdoors and sometimes indoors. Today's one is indoors."

"And the purpose of them? Is it to make money from the sale of them?"

"Oh no. Keith takes them as a hobby. He enjoys photography."

"But all the ones I've seen are of nude men. Is that all he takes?"

"What do you mean all the ones you've seen?"

"Precisely what I say. I have only seen nude guys, not that I have a problem with that, but it means that the models must be nude when he takes the photos and you're not there. Do you understand where I'm going with this?"

"No, Dad, but where have you seen these photos? I've never shown you."

"On the computer, Peter. I've seen them on a website and I've also seen ones of Keith, and then I worry that you are here with me today but he's taking nude photos of other guys, so who's to say that nothing is going on with him and the model while you're here?"

"Dad! Keith is not like that. I trust him."

"If you say so," replied Fred, shrugging his shoulders.

"And where on the computer did you see them?" Peter asked, sounding a little peeved.

"Oh, on some site like Photos.com or something like that. Haven't you seen them?"

Now it was Peter's turn to shrug his shoulders, casually.

"When we go inside I'll show you if you like."

"Dad, I don't need to see them as I see them at home, and as I say, I trust Keith."

"Sure, son, I hear you. But now tell me something, how many friends do you have?"

Peter looked perplexed at this question.

"I have plenty," he replied.

"Right, hold up your hands and using your fingers count and tell me who they are."

Peter did as he was asked, and raised both hands, spreading his fingers wide. Then he started to name his friends.

"Well, there's Gavin and Chris…"

"I said friends," interrupted Fred, "not acquaintances."

Peter looked a little stunned by this.

"Come on, count them," repeated Fred.

Peter started counting again, but this time was finding it difficult. He came to a stop when he had two fingers held up.

"Do you see what I mean? You have very few friends. Now how about Keith?"

Peter held up his open hand to count and realizing what his Dad had said, he closed it again.

"I don't think he has many, if any, when you put it like you did, Dad."

"You see Peter, I worry about you and I know you used to have many genuine friends, but where are they now?"

"Well, you know Dad, when you go into a relationship, you often lose those friends."

"But why should you Peter? They were there for you when you never had a relationship and they stood by you all the time; now that you have a relationship, do you stand by them?"

Peter looked his Dad in the eyes and then hung his head.

"All I'm concerned about is that now that you and Keith are together, are you not letting your genuine friends go, losing touch with them, ignoring them?"

"I suppose when you put it like that, you're right, Dad."

"You can lose a partner, but you mustn't lose your genuine friends, Peter. They are there for life and not just until you tire of them as you might do in a relationship. However, enough of this. Let's go inside and I'll make some lunch for us."

Fred put his arm around Peter's shoulders and led him into the house and into the kitchen where they started to prepare something to eat.

The kitchen was not small, yet it was laid out in a very compact way. The work areas were near the stove and there was an area for washing up and laundry. Fred had not lived in this house for very long. In fact, he had only been there for six months and this was only the second visit by Peter. Previously, Fred's house had been in a relatively isolated spot, but this house, which was bigger than his previous one, did have neighbors on either side of him. The house had four bedrooms and Peter had queried when he first saw it, why his father wanted such a large house when he lived alone! Fred had shrugged and said that he might enjoy having visitors.

A casual, light lunch of salads was prepared and both men settled down at the dining room table to enjoy their lunch.

"You know I mentioned earlier that I was thinking of getting a part-time job, well I was thinking of going into the real estate business," said Fred, taking a sip of his dry white wine that they were enjoying with their lunch.

"That sounds like a good idea," replied Peter, "but do you know anything about it?

"I would say I know a little but I can always learn. Obviously, there are basics to know and I am sure that each company has their own methods and procedures that I would have to learn as I would go along."

"True and I don't think it would take you long to pick up things."

"Meaning?" quipped Fred.

Peter laughed as he realised what he had said.

"Well, I suppose that could happen, too," chuckled Fred. "Tell me, who was that friend of yours who stayed the weekend with us when I was still in the old house? Wasn't he in real estate?"

"Oh yes, you mean Brad."

"He was the guy who was with that actor."

"Yes, Phil the neurotic one."

"I suppose you might call him that, but I think by the end of the weekend he wasn't too bad. Are they still together?"

"I really have no idea as I haven't seen or heard from either for quite some time."

"Oh, I thought you were very good friends with Brad and kept in touch with him."

"I did for a while and then he seemed to disappear from the scene."

"But do you have his contact number?" enquired Fred.

"Oh yes, I have that. Let me look in my bag and I'll give it to you."

"No rush, son, we can do that after lunch. Sit and enjoy your food and drink. Talking of drink, would you like something other than wine?"

"If you have a beer, that would be nice, thanks Dad."

Fred rose from the table and ambled over to the fridge, opened it and pulled out two beers, one for Peter and one for himself.

"There you go Peter," said Fred, handing him his cold, opened beer.

Peter took a swig from the bottle and smacked his lips.

"Hmm, that tastes good!" said the young man.

There was a moment of silence as both men enjoyed their lunch and beers, and then Peter broke the silence.

"Dad, don't you have a big birthday coming up soon?"

"If you say so," replied Fred, nonchalantly.

"I believe it's the big 65, isn't it?"

"Hmm, if you say so."

"Dad, stop being so casual about it. You are turning 65, aren't you?"

"Yes my boy, but that makes me sound so old."

"Look at it this way; you'll be over half a century and I'll be over a quarter of a century."

"Oh lovely! Over half a century! You do realise that not many people ever get to be a century so that makes it sound quite daunting and not much time left for me."

"But you know what I mean, and who knows, you might just make it to a century."

Fred gave Peter a rather indignant look, smiled and shook his head.

"I doubt it, but it is a nice thought, son."

"The reason that I brought up the subject was that I was thinking of organizing a party for you and inviting some of your friends along."

"Nice thought, Peter, but I don't think so."

"Why not, Dad?"

"Well, it's bound to be a rather dull party as I don't have many friends, and it would be a waste of money, too."

"I'm not listening to your excuses; I'm going to go ahead and arrange it. After all, I haven't had many chances to do things for you, so the least I can do is organize the party for you."

"Oh, and not pay for it?" quipped Fred, with a slight chuckle.

The two men sat drinking their beer and tucking into their lunch.

Peter was an only child who had led a rather awkward life being split between his mother and his father. However, as the years passed, he had developed a lasting and deep relationship with his father without losing contact with his mother. Being an only child did not necessarily mean that Peter had led a spoilt life.

As a young boy, Peter's parents always supported him in the sports arena. Whenever there was an athletic meet, Fred and Moira, his mother, were there, just as they were always at the swimming pool when Peter raced.

Fred was tall, just like Peter, and thanks to his years of swimming and sailing, he had developed broad shoulders, which tapered to a slim waist, and long, well-developed legs that extended from his Speedo. His face was one of openness with twinkling eyes and a broad smile, and on the sides of his temples were strands of distinguishing grey hair. Fred never looked his age, even though 65 was coming up soon. There were times when Peter often thought of his Dad, not as much as a father, but a close friend or brother. Fred was young-hearted and he achieved this by encouraging Peter to visit him with his friends. In fact, it was on one of these visits that Peter brought his coach, Patrick to stay for the weekend, and it was over that weekend that Fred and Patrick realised that they had a warm connection. After that first meeting, the two older men saw each other regularly and Patrick spent many weekends in the company of Fred. The love for each other grew stronger, and this made Peter happy, knowing that his Dad had someone special in his life. Unfortunately, Patrick took a transfer to another college and that meant their seeing each other came to a halt. Over time, they realised the difficulty of a long-distance relationship and decided to go their separate ways. However, Fred still had a longing for Patrick even though they had not seen each other for quite some time, and had heard rumors that Patrick was seeing someone else.

"Dad, do you have any special invitations you want sent for your birthday? Any special friends you want invited?" asked Peter, breaking the silence.

"No, son. I have not actually thought of anything along those lines, but I really do not want anything special. Maybe just you and a couple of your friends would be fine."

"But they would be my friends and not yours, and in any case, you might not even know some of them."

"Not a problem, as I can get to know them," answered Fred. "I'll leave it all up to you, Peter."

They finished their lunch and Fred collected the dishes and placed them in the kitchen to wash later.

"Another beer, Peter?" asked Fred, grabbing a bottle for himself from the fridge.

"Sure, thanks Dad."

Fred took another beer from the fridge and handed it to Peter and the two men went back outside to lie next to the swimming pool.

"Are you going to stay the night, son?" enquired Fred.

"I hadn't planned on staying, Dad, but I'll see how I feel later. I don't have to go back home tonight as I have nothing planned."

"Well, it would be nice if you stayed the night. Even though I do have neighbors around and I see them more than I saw neighbors in the old house, I do not often have people stay over."

Both men swam, drank their beers and chatted with each other until the sun began to set over the sea and Fred asked Peter again if he was going to stay the night.

"If you don't mind, Dad."

"I did invite you and there's plenty of room here."

"But I think I'd better phone Keith to let him know," answered Peter.

They finished their beers and watched the sun sink slowly under the horizon and all that was left was the orange glow in the sky and just as slowly, they could feel the air around them begin to cool, forcing them to return indoors and strip off their Speedos and pull on a pair of shorts each.

CHAPTER 2

"Use the landline to phone Keith, Peter," said Fred.

Peter dialed the number and waited while the phone at the other end rang. It was picked up and Peter heard Keith's voice.

"Hi Keith, it's Peter here. I think I've had a bit too much beer to drink and could be a risk if I try driving home, so I'm going to stay at my Dad's place tonight and then drive home tomorrow morning."

"No problem, Honey."

"How did the photo shoot go?"

"Great. He was a good model, very natural," replied Keith.

Fred stood close by but was unable to hear everything.

"He said he would like to do another session," continued Keith, "but he wants to do some outdoor shots this time."

"Oh, that sounds nice. Have you set up a date with him?"

Fred's face looked alarmed when he heard that last comment. He indicated that he wanted to speak to Keith.

"Hey Keith, my Dad wants to say 'Hi' to you. Hang on."

Peter handed the receiver to Fred.

"Hi Keith, it's Fred here."

"Hi Fred. Sorry I could not make it to your place but I had this appointment today."

"Not a problem, Keith. Who was the model?"

"I placed some adverts in the media and he was one of them who replied. I did get some other interested parties but when I arranged for them to come for a shoot, they did not pitch up; real nuisance when that happens. This guy was a real natural, as I was telling Peter."

"That sounds really great," replied Fred, trying to think of what to say next.

"I should do a session with you, Fred," said Keith laughing.

"You're not serious, are you?"

"I'm absolutely serious. For a guy of your age, you have a really great, well-defined body…"

Fred burst out laughing, which made Peter look aghast and wonder what Keith had said.

"I think we should make a date and maybe give the photos to Peter as a present."

Fred thought that it did sound like a good idea – the present idea – but he was not sure about posing naked for Keith.

"I'll think about it, Keith and let you know, but in the meantime, I'll look after Peter tonight. You just take it easy tonight too," said Fred, handing the receiver back to Peter.

"Hi Keith, what are you and my Dad plotting?"

"Nothing serious."

"It sounded funny whatever it was."

"I just suggested that your Dad should do a photo shoot."

At that, Peter also burst into laughter.

"You're joking aren't you?" he enquired of Keith.

"Not at all. I think he could be good."

Peter was still laughing heartily when he and Keith finished their conversation and he had replaced the receiver again. Peter looked at his Dad from head to foot and laughed some more.

"What's so funny, son?" asked Fred.

"I'm trying to visualize you posing for Keith and him taking photos of you."

"Hey, buddy. I might be reaching 65, but I still have a good body."

"I know," answered Peter. "It's just that I can't imagine you doing it," he continued, still laughing with glee.

As Peter continued to speak, Fred sat admiring his son and thinking of how he had turned into such a handsome young man. Peter had inherited his mother's facial features of a full mouth with an enigmatic smile, high cheekbones, while he had gained his father's masculinity. His face, tanned as a Greek's might look, showed sensitivity and child-like quality that belied his age, and his muscular physique was well developed and defined. His soft green eyes seemed to glisten as he spoke to Keith, and when he laughed, his full lips parted, revealing a set of pure white teeth. In Fred's eyes, Peter was truly handsome.

"Now tell me what were you and Keith discussing that had you in fits of laughter?" Peter asked his father.

"Oh, he had some silly idea to photograph me."

"Well I think it's a good idea. You have a really hot body for a guy of your age and I think you would look good in the photos too."

"But for what purpose?" enquired Fred.

"Hey, Dad, you said you wanted to get a part-time job so maybe you could go in for modeling."

With that, Fred roared with laughter thinking of the impossibility of him modeling.

"You are joking aren't you? And what am I going to model for?"

"Could be anything, clothing, facial shots or products. I do not know specifically, but you really are well kept for someone your age and I know there are products on the market to keep people looking young and you do look young."

Peter admired how his father had managed to stay looking so young and inwardly also hoped that when he got older, he too would retain his youthful vigor and looks.

"Give it a try, Dad; you've got nothing to lose by letting Keith take some shots of you."

"I'll think about it, son," replied Fred, still chuckling to himself at the thought. "By the way, how old is Keith? I don't think you've ever told me."

"Forty-six this year," answered Peter.

"Hmm! You like older men, I see!" commented Fred with a wry smile on his face.

"I suppose you could say that. I just think they are more mature and know what they want in life. Not like some of the younger guys who only want sex and nothing else."

"But what is your relationship with Keith built around?" questioned Fred.

"What do you mean, Dad?"

"Well, are you both monogamous or what?"

"We have an open relationship but within limits."

"Meaning?"

"Well, we agreed to see other guys but together. What I mean is that we would only go with another guy if both of us were with the guy. It's not part of the deal that I or Keith can just pick up a guy for fun without the other being present."

Fred sat silent for a moment, listening intently, figuring out what Peter had just explained to him.

"So correct me if I'm wrong; what you're saying is that, say, you two guys go to a bar and you meet someone there you would both go with…"

"… Yes…"

"… But neither Keith nor you would pick up a guy in the bar and have sex with him without the other being there or knowing about it?" asked Fred.

"Being there, Dad," replied Peter.

"So in other words it could happen, and I say *could*, that one of you might have sex with another guy and not tell the partner?"

"I suppose when you put it that way, yes."

"So then I don't understand your interpretation of an open relationship. To me it sounds a matter of convenience, or even hypocrisy. Let's pretend that I'm a guy in a bar and you come in on your own and I make advances towards you and suggest that we go to the back room, if there is one, or to the toilet for a bit of sex, and you agree. When you get home do you tell Keith?"

"Well no, it wouldn't happen."

"Do you mean telling Keith or having sex in the toilet?"

"Having sex in the toilet!"

"Okay, let's say it wasn't in a toilet but in some luxurious bedroom?"

"No, Dad, I still wouldn't do it."

"And Keith?"

"I'm sure he wouldn't either."

"But if both of you came into the bar and I made a pass at you and Keith was there, then what?"

"If I fancied you, both he and I would discuss it and see if he also fancied you, then we'd both agree to go to the toilet with you for some sex."

Fred smiled slightly as his mind worked out what Peter had just said to him.

"But what if you fancied me and Keith didn't, yet he was with you, then what?"

"Well if that scenario arose, we'd both go with you either to the toilet or to your luxurious bedroom and I would have sex with you and Keith would just watch."

"Kinky!" exclaimed Fred with a broad smile, to which Peter also chuckled loudly. "Well I hope that you both stick to this arrangement and neither one gets hurt in any way."

"I think we're good, Dad. We understand each other's likes and dislikes and I'm sure that neither of us will go behind the other's back and do anything that might harm our relationship."

"I hope that you're right, my boy."

"Are you happier now Dad?"

"Listen, Peter, you know how much I care for you and I wouldn't want you hurt in any way, so that's why I ask these questions. If I didn't care about you, I wouldn't have asked or become worried about your relationship. Do you understand?"

"I do Dad, and I respect your care and love for me, and I think you know that if anything happened between Keith and me, I would tell you about it. Now tell me, what are we eating tonight?"

"Ah, Dinner! What about take out pizzas?"

"Sounds good to me," replied Peter. "Can I phone an order through?"

"Sure. Get me whatever you're ordering and while you do that, I'm going to get under the shower."

Fred left the lounge and went to his bedroom to shower in the en suite bathroom while Peter placed the pizza orders.

"Is there anything you want to do tonight?" shouted Fred from the bedroom.

"Not really," replied Peter, shouting back. "Anything you want to do, Dad?"

The water was rushing in the shower so Fred never heard Peter's question. Peter went through to the master bedroom and into the bathroom where his Dad was showering.

"I asked if there was anything that you would like to do, Dad," remarked Peter, seeing his Dad's V-shaped chest and strong legs along with his firm butt.

Fred turned to face his son.

"Sorry, what was that Peter?"

"I just asked if there was something that you might want to do?"

Fred shook his head and carried on soaping his muscular torso.

Peter could not take his eyes off his Dad. Here was a man turning 65 with the body of a 20- or 30-year-old, trim, strong and good to look at.

"You know Dad, you could get any man you wanted with that body of yours."

Fred laughed and then added, "The physical isn't everything you know, Peter. You could have the most magnificent body and the dullest brain and believe me that would not be worth living with for all the money in the world. No, I'm happy the way I am at the moment."

"I'm glad that you added 'at the moment' as I was beginning to think that you were never going to look at another man again."

Fred smiled at his son's concern for him.

"You don't have to worry about me. If Mr. Right comes along, I'll do something about it, but until then, I'll just enjoy life as it is."

He switched off the faucet, stepped out of the shower and grabbed a towel to dry himself.

"Why the sudden concern, Peter?" enquired Fred.

"It's not sudden, Dad. It's that I care for you and worry about you, even if you didn't think that I did."

Fred smiled warmly at Peter.

"I know you do, son, and I'm very grateful for that. After Patrick left, I think I became a little empty inside, but I think I've got over it now."

Peter knew that there had been a strong bond between his former sports coach Patrick and his Dad.

"That's why I think I need to get a part-time job of some sort so that I can keep myself occupied and maybe meet other people at the same time."

"Well, if you go into the property business, I'm sure that you'll be meeting people on a daily basis. That reminds me, I must give you Brad's telephone number."

"Yes, please, Peter, then I can phone him tomorrow morning."

Fred finished drying himself and slipped on a pair of running shorts, which showed off his massive endowment proudly, and then made his way back into the lounge, with Peter following.

The front doorbell rang and Fred went to open the door. The pizza delivery man stood there with two large boxes.

"Hi, how much do I owe you?" asked Fred, rummaging in his wallet for money.

The pizza man, who looked to be in his very early 20s, eyed Fred intently. Peter could see how the young man's eyes travelled from Fred's face over the buffed chest and came to an abrupt halt when he saw the bulge and elongated outline of Fred's heavy cock in his running shorts. Fred smiled when he noticed the young man transfixed by what he saw, so he nonchalantly lowered his hand to brush across the front of his shorts as if to entice the young man.

"How much do I owe you, son?" enquired Fred with a rather enigmatic smile on his face.

The young man mumbled "30 dollars, sir," but never even glanced up at Fred. He remained in a hypnotic state.

Fred handed him a $50 bill and added, "There's a nice big tip for you."

The young man's face never moved.

"I can see that, sir," he replied, his eyes still transfixed on the bulge.

Peter, guffawed on hearing this comment, but Fred remained stoic, took the pizza boxes in one hand and with his other gave his heavy penis a squeeze. The young pizza man's jaw dropped and his mouth gaped open much like a fish gulping for air while his eyes remained fixed on the treasure that he had just observed.

"Good night, son, and thanks for the pizzas," said Fred, closing the front door.

Fred turned to Peter who was sitting in the lounge watching the whole scenario and smiled at his son.

"At least I brought some happiness to that young man."

"I can assure you Dad, that he'll want to deliver pizzas here on a regular basis," laughed Peter.

The two men tucked into their pizzas with gusto, chatting about the young man's facial expression on seeing how well Fred was endowed.

"Tell me Dad, have you heard from Patrick at all lately?"

"No son. I often wonder how he's getting on in life and what he's up to."

"Have you not phoned him at all?"

"You know it's funny, I have been tempted to but never really had the courage to do so. I do not know why; after all, we never parted as enemies. He has also not phoned me so I think it was like a way for him to make the break clean so as to get on with his life."

"But what are your feelings about him, Dad?"

"Peter, I still think he's a smart chap, good looking and great in bed, but he wanted to move on so it was only right that I let him go. I always say that if you let a bird fly away and it comes back, then it was never meant to leave in the first place. If at some later stage Patrick wants to come back to me, I might take him back, but we will have to cross that bridge when we come to it. I'll always have a soft spot in my heart for him, as he brought a great deal of happiness into my life."

"I liked him and I thought he was so good for you," commented Peter, taking the last slice of his pizza and closing the box.

"Oh, for sure he was good for me. He brought a lot out of me; my enthusiasm for life was rejuvenated and my loneliness disappeared. Yes, he was a great guy all round, and yes, I do miss him, but you cannot hold someone back if he wants to better his life or career."

Fred seemed to have a distant look on his face as if reliving the times he had with Patrick, and Peter could see that his father was deep in thought about the man he used to love. At the same time, Peter began to think of Keith and their relationship. He knew that Keith had enjoyed a couple of relationships with other men in the past and had, according to Keith, broken up with these men because they tended to "play around" while in the relationship with Keith. Peter had never questioned Keith's allegations but he had no reason to do so at this moment in time. It did however cross his mind, the comments that his Dad had made and the questions that he had asked about Keith.

"What are you thinking of?" questioned Fred, after a while of silence.

"Oh, nothing much," replied Peter. "Hey, before I forget, let me give you Brad's telephone number, Dad."

Peter rose from the sofa and collected his address book from his backpack that he had brought along with him.

"Here it is, Dad," said Peter, writing the number down on a piece of paper for his father, and handing it to him.

"Thanks, son. I'll give him a call in the morning and see what he has to say about your old man taking on a part-time job."

"I don't know about you, Dad, but I think the beers from this afternoon and the pizza have made me a bit sleepy. Do you mind if I excuse myself and head to bed?"

"I think I'll do the same," replied Fred, stretching and yawning at the same time. "It's been a great day Peter and it was so nice to see you again. You should visit more often and come and see your poor old Dad."

Peter chuckled and added, "Not so much of the old! You're still a spring chicken and don't forget what you've always said to me, that age is a state of mind, so I don't want to ever hear you saying that you're old again!"

Fred grinned at the telling off that he had received from Peter and said, "Yes sir! Whenever in your presence, I promise not to mention the 'old' word again."

CHAPTER 3

Fred dialed the number that Peter had given him and waited to hear the ringing on the other end of the line. Fred heard a phone receiver be picked up and then a male voice spoke.

"Brad Johnson speaking, how may I help you?"

"Hello Brad. I don't know if you remember me but it's Fred Summers speaking. I'm Peter's Dad."

"Oh yes," replied Brad sounding unsure of the speaker on the other end of the line.

"You spent a weekend at my old house with Peter and a few other friends. Do you remember now?"

"Oh, yes, now I do. Hi Mr. Summers, nice to hear from you again. How are you and how's Peter been?"

"I'm fine thanks Brad, and so is Peter. In fact, he has just left here to go back home. He spent the night with me. I think he had a bit too much to drink," continued Fred, laughing as he explained why Peter had stayed the night.

"I haven't spoken to Peter for some time now, but I did hear that he was in a relationship."

"Yes, with an older guy called Keith. I don't know if you've heard of him or know him?"

"I'm not sure that I do, but if I know more details, I might know him," answered Brad.

"And tell me, are you still with your boyfriend, what's his name…?"

"Phil," remarked Brad. "No, we broke up soon after we left your place. I think it was about a couple of weeks later and we went our different ways."

"I'm sorry to hear that. I was hoping that you and Phil might have patched things up."

"No such luck. I think Phil got tired of my chasing hot guys," laughed Brad.

"So, am I to take it that you're still chasing hot guys, hey Brad?"

"You've hit the nail on the head, Mr. Summers. But tell me what can I do for you?"

"Brad, I was telling Peter last night that I was thinking of taking on a part-time job if I could get one, to keep me occupied and out of mischief as you might say!"

"So how does that affect me?"

"I was wondering if you needed any extra staff in the property business to help out on a part-time basis."

"Well, we're always looking for good agents, but as you've had no real experience, it might be a bit of a problem, but I'm sure that we could discuss something. Would you like me to have a chat with you over some coffee and see what we can come up with that might be convenient to both you and me?"

"That would be great, Brad, I appreciate it. When would it suit you to meet? If you are pushed for time, you could come round to my place."

"That sounds better," replied Brad. "Are you still staying in the same house?"

"No. It is in the same suburb but I am at 18 Ravenswood Place. Do you know where that is?"

"I'll find it. What time would suit you, Mr. Summers?"

"I'm in your hands, Brad. I have all day free so you say what time suits you instead."

"How would it be if I came to you about 3 P.M. this afternoon? I will be finished for the day so we would not have to rush things," said Brad.

"Sounds great to me. Look forward to seeing you again, Brad."

"Same here, Mr. Summers."

As Fred replaced the telephone receiver, he smiled, thinking about how good it would be to work again and see people on a daily basis. Although he had no experience in selling property, he felt sure that he knew enough about interior decor to determine the potential of a property. Fred promptly telephoned Peter to tell him that Brad was coming around for a meeting later in the day. Fred spent the rest of the day tanning next to his swimming pool and thinking about his future.

At precisely 3pm, a very smart, black Mercedes-Benz arrived outside of his house and the front doorbell rang. Fred, who had changed after his swimming into a pair of casual shorts and a T-shirt, opened the front door to allow Brad entry.

Brad still had the making of a junior Mr. Universe with his biceps bulging from the tight short-sleeved shirt that he was wearing, and his thighs bulging magnificently in the smart, casual jeans he was wearing.

"Hi Mr. Summers," said Brad, extending a hand and shaking hands with Fred.

"Hi Brad, how are you? Oh and please, call me Fred. Come in," said Fred ushering Brad in and closing the front door behind him. "Come through to the lounge."

Brad followed Fred as he led the way into the lounge with its scenic view across the swimming pool towards the sea.

"When did you move into this house, Fred? I thought that you were still in the other house."

"I think it was quite some time after you had visited. I just decided to move closer to some civilization if you want to put it that way.

Please have a seat, Brad. Can I offer you something to drink: tea, coffee, something stronger?"

"Whatever you're having, thanks Fred."

"I thought I would have a beer. Would you like one too?"

"That sounds great," replied Brad. "I notice you still have that magnificent view of the sea from here like you had in your old house," shouted Brad from the lounge as Fred had gone to the kitchen to fetch their beers.

"Yes," shouted Fred. "I can't do without the sight or sound of the sea."

Fred reentered the lounge with two beers and glasses along with a few snacks.

"Here we go Brad, can I pour for you?"

"Thanks Fred," answered Brad moving back to the sofa and sitting down.

"Help yourself to some snacks if you're hungry."

"I think I'll pass on the snacks, thanks Fred, but the beer is beautifully cold for a day like today. Cheers!"

"Yeah, cheers, Brad," replied Fred. "So tell me, are you still with your friend, Phil?"

"No, but we are still friends."

"Oh, I'm sorry that you went your own ways, as I thought Phil was quite a sweet guy."

"He is, yes."

"So what's Phil doing? Still in the acting trade?" enquired Fred.

"Yes. He's actually doing a show that opens in about two week's time," replied Brad.

"That's great for him, and what about you? Anyone in your life, Brad?"

"I met someone else and we had a bit of a fling together, but now I'm single again."

Fred chuckled and added, "You haven't changed, have you?"

Brad chuckled back, knowing exactly to what Fred was referring.

"You mean the boyfriends, hey!"

"Yes, I do. You sure go through the guys don't you?" continued Fred, smiling at the younger man and sitting down in a wingback chair opposite Brad.

"And what about you, Fred? Any man in your life? I did hear about Patrick leaving to go elsewhere."

"No, no one at the moment, but that doesn't mean that the door has been closed."

"Well, I'm glad that you're still on the market, so to speak," said Brad with a broad grin. "I'm sure you'll get someone very quickly as you still have so much going for you – you're still very handsome, have a super trim body, from what I can see, and those firm legs of yours..."

Fred looked down at his legs, which were spread widely.

"... I've always admired those legs of yours."

"Well thanks Brad, but you still look incredibly good. Are you still going to the gym?"

"Almost every day in between appointments, if I can make it."

"Well I can see it's paying off."

Fred knew that Brad liked to be admired by all, young and old and Brad had always been prone to preening himself but in a good way. Fred did acknowledge that for his age, Brad was good looking and had taken care of his physical appearance and maybe that was part of Brad's problem of keeping relationships. Fred remembered the weekend that Peter, along with Brad and their friends had stayed at Fred's house. It had been where there had been any amount of drama not only as a result of Brad's hormones having a good time, but also because of the arrival of James, an unexpected visitor who was later arrested for fraud and harassing Fred's ex-wife in a ploy to get at Fred.

"Do you remember that story that James related to us the day the police arrested him?" asked Fred.

"Sort of," answered Brad rather sheepishly.

"The reason I ask this is that I wondered if you had changed in any way."

"I don't really know."

"Remember that James had told of the tribe who lived in the forest. They had spent their entire lives within the darkness of the forest, but one day, one of their members had suggested that they venture out of their particular area and go to see if there was any other life around them. A group of men took their meager defenses with them such as bows and arrows and a spear or two, and they pushed their way through the trees and bush until they came to an opening on the edge of the forest. They hesitated in the safety of the forest and surveyed the area ahead of them. There was open land, but this open land was bright, unlike the world they had come from, and seemed to be lit by something bright high up in the heavens. Their eyes were blinded when they looked up at this bright yellow-gold object, but they decided to advance slowly into the open area. As they did so, they were overcome by intense warmth, which seemed to emanate from this bright object above them, and then fear overcame them. They noticed on the ground that there were dark objects, which resembled their shapes, and they started to shoot their arrows and throw their spears at these moving images, but they continued to move. In terror, the men hurried back into the safety of the dark forest, with the images following them. When they entered their realm, they noticed that the dark images did not follow them in, so they felt a little safer. Curiosity, however, got the better of some of them, and again they ventured out to see if the bright object and its dark images were still there and to see whether these images had in fact died from their weapons. Slowly they crept to the verge of the forest and once again noticed that the dark images had returned, so they fled once more into the forest and they remained there for the rest of their lives, knowing that the images were not with them."

Brad had remained transfixed on Fred as he retold the story. He wondered why Fred was telling him this, but he waited for Fred to finish.

"And do you remember what else he told you?"

Brad shook his head. "Not everything, Fred."

"Well, he said that you should be the one to come to terms with the shadow which is attached to you. Not only were you false to others, but you were being false to yourself. Do you remember that?"

"Yes, now I remember," said Brad still looking a little sheepish.

"He said that you shouldn't have to try to con people into liking you or try to buy their affections. He said that you wanted to be Peter Pan and have everlasting youth, but to remember that in the story of Peter Pan, he also lost his shadow. Now it was time for you to do likewise if you wanted to have a real, genuine relationship with anyone. Do you remember all that?"

"I sure do, Fred, and I think I have changed for the better."

"I hope so, Brad. The reason I raised that whole issue is that I want to get into the property business and I would like to work with you in your company. However, I want to know that I can trust you and that even if you do have relationships that have nothing to do with me, that it is not going to impact on the company or on our working relationship. It's not that I want to lay down the rules, but I like to be professional in my work environment."

"I promise, Fred, that I have changed and I don't let my love life interfere with my work environment or vice versa."

"I'm glad to hear that. Now tell me about your company and whether you think I would fit in there providing of course you want to offer me part-time work," said Fred, now smiling enigmatically at Brad.

"I would love to work with you, Fred, because you are levelheaded and mature and we need someone like that in the company. You see, all the others there are young or at least around my age, so sometimes things do get a little out of hand."

"Meaning?" enquired Fred.

"Well, I'm sure you know how younger people get sometimes over a weekend and then on a Monday there are a few sore heads…"

"… And that impacts on the work, does it?" asked Fred.

"Yes, you could say that," chuckled Brad.

"Listen, I don't have a problem with you guys having fun over a weekend, so long as your Mondays don't impact on me when I'm trying to work."

"Oh no, never, Fred. That would never happen. I'd see to it that nobody in that state bothered you."

Fred looked long and hard at Brad to ascertain if he was being genuine or not.

"I want the work to keep me occupied and to meet new people, but I still want to work in a serious manner," said Fred in a fatherly tone.

Brad, for some reason also felt that it was like his father speaking to him and he listened intently. He knew in his heart that having Fred in the company would be the best thing for him, not only to keep an eye on him and to keep him under control, but for the company to have an older person was also good for business. He had realised that many clients were not young and when dealing with some of his staff, he felt the clients dismissed the younger sales staff more easily than they might when dealing with an older person.

"Fred, when would you like to start?" asked Brad.

"You haven't even discussed contracts with me or finances."

Brad roared with laughter. "You see how eager I am for you to be in the company, I didn't even think of those things. I'll tell you what, let me set up an appointment for you with our finance section and they can go over all the commission details and what you would be expected to do in the company, but I will speak to them first, explaining how I see you fitting into the company. Is that fine with you?"

"Absolutely," replied Fred, somewhat happy without actually showing it. "Now, would you like another beer and maybe even a swim?"

"I thought you were never going to offer the beer, but as for the swim, I haven't come prepared for that."

"Not a problem in this house. You should know that. I have a number of Speedos you could wear or if you're really adventurous, we can skinny dip!"

"Well, that's entirely up to you," laughed Brad, "but a Speedo will do fine thanks, Fred."

"Size?" asked Fred, rising from the sofa and about to head to his bedroom.

"Well that depends on what you've got, after all, you aren't a clothing store."

"It's easier if you come with me and try some on then."

Both men headed off to Fred's bedroom and Brad was soon stripped and trying on various Speedos until he found one that fitted him.

"How does that feel?" Fred enquired, admiring the firm butt and the hefty bulge in the front of the Speedo.

"A bit tight," replied Brad, "but I think I'll be fine, thanks."

"There is a size slightly bigger," said Fred, "to accommodate that huge package that you're carrying."

They both laughed at Fred's comment and Brad unconsciously felt his bulge and tried to rearrange it in the Speedo.

"I think I should be fine as it's only us there in the pool, so if it gets a bit awkward I can always slip it off," replied Brad.

"Absolutely," answered Fred, handing Brad a towel to use at the pool. "Bring your beer and let's head out to the pool."

The two men went out into the warm sunshine and placed their beers on the table that was situated under a larger umbrella. They then dived simultaneously into the cool, refreshing water. Brad surfaced first and swam a little distance to the opposite side from where he had dived in. In a matter of seconds, Fred surfaced next to him and rested his arms on the edge of the pool.

"Mm, this is refreshing," said Brad, shaking the excess water from his hair. "Wow! It's nice to get away from the office and relax here," he added.

"Well, when I start work with you, we can always take some time off to come for a swim if the boss allows it," said Fred with a wink of the eye and a smirk across his face.

They stayed at the edge in the water, chatting casually about everyday things until Brad asked Fred about Peter and his relationship with Keith.

"The way you asked how they were doing sounded a little suspect to me, if I may say," commented Fred, "Also when I spoke to you, you said you weren't sure if you knew Keith."

"I gave it some thought afterwards and realised that there was only one Keith that either I or Peter might know. I just wondered if things were still as good as when they first went into their relationship."

"As far as I know, things seem fine," said Fred, anxious to know more about Brad's asking of the relationship. "I did wonder for a time, but Peter assures me that all is super."

Brad nodded and smiled, but Fred was concerned that the smile seemed too artificial.

"What are you hiding, Brad? What do you know that I don't?"

"I have no idea what you do know," he retorted.

"All I know is that Keith does photography as a hobby and they seem to be getting along just fine, that is according to Peter."

"I don't know if you are aware that Keith and I had a fling together."

"No, I wasn't aware of that. Was that before Peter that you and he got together or during his relationship with Peter?"

"No, before. We met in a pub one night and he asked if I would model for him and I agreed, thinking it might be in underwear or a Speedo or something like that."

"And?"

"Well, when we got back to his place, it became clear to me that the photography was secondary. Yes, we did a few shots in my underwear, and then he asked if I would strip for him, which I did. He took a number of pictures of me in various poses, and then asked if I would like to look at a porn magazine – obviously to arouse me. I started looking at the various pictures which were of guys fucking, and naturally I did become aroused, and that's when the photography took on a totally different meaning. He stripped off too, and was playing with himself while snapping pictures. He then set the camera down and got a video camera, set that up and then asked me to fuck him."

"He wanted you to fuck him?"

"Yes."

"But he wasn't in a relationship, was he?"

"That's the interesting part – he was. Unbeknown to me, his boyfriend had gone out that evening."

"And so what happened?"

"Well, he could see how aroused I was, so he started feeling me up, and naturally it felt good so I let him continue, and then he lay down, raised his legs, and wanted me to fuck him."

"And I take it that you did?"

"Yes. When we had finished, he got up off the floor where we had been and switched off the video camera. I had forgotten that it was still running, and then he said he would have to hide it from his boyfriend. That is when I found out he was in a relationship.

"What did you do, Brad?"

"I was a little shocked but the problem was that I felt sexually happy and fulfilled, so truthfully, I had mixed feelings. Then he played back some of the video and that made us both horny again, watching ourselves at it."

"I'm assuming that you're going to tell me that you went for round two!" enquired Fred.

Brad merely smiled coyly, making Fred realise that he had. It also made Fred wonder if the same thing was happening when Peter was at his place or visiting friends.

"Brad, may I ask for your opinion?"

"Sure, Fred."

"Do you think that Keith might be doing the same to Peter?"

"Hey, that I can't say, but if he did it with me while his partner was out, who's to say he won't be doing it with some other guy when Peter isn't around!"

Fred shook his head almost in disbelief at what he had heard. Nothing more was said and both men began to swim a couple of lengths and then stopping to catch their breath once they got to the steps leading into the swimming pool. Fred sat on the steps leading into the water and watched Brad continue to swim a couple more lengths. Brad finally came to a halt and rested on the step next to Fred.

"Pretty fit, hey!" commented Fred, patting his new boss on the shoulder.

"I try to stay fit."

"To keep up with the other guys, or to attract the other guys?"

"Both!" laughed Brad.

They sat there for sometime enjoying the descending sun's rays on them and then Brad rose and said, "I suppose I should be going."

Fred looked up at the young muscular body standing next to him. Fred's face was in line with the massive bulge that seemed desperate to break free from the tight Speedo. His mind flashed back to Patrick and the fun times they had together and seemed to go into a thoughtful trance. Brad became aware of the way that Fred was staring at his crotch. He never said a word, but allowed the older man the pleasure of admiring what was before him. Brad never knew what was going through Fred's mind, but he enjoyed the amount of attention that his bulge seemed to be getting.

Eventually, Brad placed a hand on the bulge, gave it a squeeze and said in a low voice to Fred, "Do you want this?"

Fred suddenly came back to reality.

"Oh, I'm sorry Brad, my mind was miles away," stammered Fred, averting his look and focusing on Brad's face.

Brad's hand remained on his crotch.

"I asked if you wanted this," Brad repeated.

"Uhm! Aagh! It really is a lovely sight Brad and I know how proud you are of your hefty manhood, but I don't think I should be playing with my future boss."

Brad's hand left his crotch and he placed it on Fred's shoulder.

"Maybe not today," said Brad, patting Fred on the shoulder and encouraging him to stand up. "I think I should be going, Fred, so let's get dressed."

Fred and Brad went back into the house and both stripped off their Speedos and got dressed. As they did so, Fred took the advantage of glancing at the naked Brad and mentally admiring the long, thick appendage that hung loosely between Brad's thighs. Fred knew that he had a reputation for being well hung, but to look at Brad made Fred think back to his own younger days and how he too had paid enormous attention to his physical appearance and how it had stood him in good stead. In fact, his well-defined body won him Peter's mother. He wondered if his physical appearance might now win over a man to bring some joy into his life.

Brad finished getting dressed and thanked Fred for the beers and the swim.

"Fred, I'll contact you tomorrow so you can come in and meet the crew and ask any questions about the contract and finances."

"Thanks Brad. I really appreciate the offer and I'm sure it's going to be great fun working with you," said Fred, shaking Brad's hand, but pulling him closer to him so as to hug him.

The two men hugged each other and then broke free.

"Cheers Fred, speak to you tomorrow."

"Cheers Brad," replied Fred as Brad closed the Mercedes-Benz car door, started up his car and sped off, rather dramatically.

Fred went back into the lounge and picked up the glass of beer he had been drinking and settled back on the sofa. He stared out of the lounge window into the darkness, which had now fallen over the sea and thought about the afternoon's events. He was content in the silence of the house, deep in thought, when the shrill ring of the telephone brought him suddenly back to reality. He quickly shot from the sofa and picked up the receiver.

"Hello, Fred speaking."

"Hi Dad, it's Peter. How's your day been?"

"Oh, hi Peter. Brad has just left. He came around to speak to me about the part-time work and I think it is going to be a good move for me. I'm actually looking forward to joining his company and I think that he's keen to have me there."

Peter laughed.

"I'm sure that he only offered you the job so he could try and get you into bed with him."

"You know, you are so wicked. Brad isn't that bad. He offered me the job because, as he said, I add maturity to the company as most of the staff appears to be young."

"And you believe him, hey Dad?" chuckled Peter.

"Why shouldn't I?"

"Did he make a pass at you while he was there?"

"And if he did, what's it to you?"

"So he did. I knew it! That's typical Brad."

"Well, let's look at it from another perspective. If he did make a pass at me, then that's a feather in my cap to show that I still have sex appeal, especially to younger guys."

Peter remained silent for a moment and then laughed heartily.

"You didn't have sex with him, did you?"

"No, Peter, I didn't and even if I had I wouldn't tell you," replied Fred with a slight supercilious tone to his voice. "They are going to contact me tomorrow to go in and look at the contract and give me all the finance details, so very soon your Dad will be working his butt off again."

"I'm really proud of you Dad and I genuinely wish you all the best in the job."

"Thanks, son. So what have you two been doing this afternoon?"

"Nothing. Just chilling at home. We're having friends around for dinner tonight so I have to prepare for them."

"That sounds good. Do I know them?"

"No Dad. They're a couple of guys who are very into nude

dinners."

"Nude dinners!" exclaimed Fred. "Isn't that a bit dangerous? I mean, what if something hot lands in the wrong place?"

"Well, we just make sure that it doesn't."

"Do you and Keith also do this nude thing?"

"Yes, but it was actually these two friends who got us into it. I will give you an update later when they have gone. In the meantime, I just wanted to know if Brad had contacted you. Glad everything seems to be going well, Dad. I'll touch sides with you later."

"O.K., my boy, but if it's very late, then phone me in the morning."

With that Fred replaced the telephone receiver and shook his head.

"Nude dinner," muttered Fred, "now I've heard everything."

CHAPTER 4

The following morning, Fred received a call from Brad informing of his meeting with the finance personnel; showered; pulled on some casual, but smart clothes, and drove to the venue. When he arrived at Brad's company building, he was pleasantly surprised how modern, up market and elegant the interior was. He approached the reception desk and a charming young lady asked if she could help him.

"Morning, my name is Fred Summers and I have an appointment…"

"… Oh yes, Mr. Summers, we were expecting you. Please have a seat and I'll call Alyson, who's in charge of finance."

Fred made himself comfortable and did not have long to wait when a tall, blonde woman in her early thirties approached him and introduced herself as Alyson.

"Pleased to meet you, Alyson, I'm Fred Summers. I believe Brad spoke to you about me."

"Please come this way, Mr. Summers," said Alyson, leading the way to her office.

"Please call me Fred," he said, as he was ushered into the comfortable office with its soft chairs and glass desk.

"Okay, Fred," said Alyson, sitting opposite Fred at the glass desk. "Brad said that you wanted to do part-time work with us, is that right?"

"Yes. I felt I needed to get out more and earn a little extra income and for some reason I thought that the property business might be my forte," remarked Fred, smiling sweetly at Alyson, who returned the sweet smile.

"May I ask how old you are Fred?"

"Pick a number! My son keeps telling me that I don't look my age," laughed Fred.

He could see that Alyson was not enamored by his sense of humor, so he quickly gave her the answer she wanted.

"Currently sixty-four."

"Thank you," she replied writing it down on a form she had in front of her. "And any previous experience in the property business?"

"None!" answered Fred, now realizing that the joking was over.

"How many days per week were you wanting to work, Fred?"

"I thought maybe two or three."

Alyson seemed very authoritarian and Fred was now beginning to wonder if he had done the right thing as he would eventually have to work with her and he was not sure that his jovial personality was going to fit into Alyson's domain.

"Hmm! That is somewhat awkward Fred, as we really need people on a full-time basis. You see, if we were to offer you something on a part-time basis it would mean both coming into the office and working here or when we have a show day presentation, you might have to attend that."

Fred was silent. He did not really want an office-bound job and he thought that being on show might only happen once a week and that was not what he really wanted.

"Tell me Alyson, do you not have any agents who might need an assistant to help them?"

"Not at the moment, I'm afraid."

Fred wondered why Brad had said that he could find him something in the company and now Alyson said there was really nothing. He sat staring at Alyson, thinking of his future, while she stared back at him without a trace of a smile. Eventually Fred rose from his soft, comfortable chair.

"I'll have to think about this, Alyson, but thank you for your time."

"You're welcome Fred," she replied, very matter-of-fact.

"I can find my own way out, thanks," said Fred, smiling curtly at Alyson, and departed from the office.

Alyson never stood up nor did she follow him out.

Fred went out into the sunlight, still a little bewildered and made his way to his car. He climbed in and drove to the beach where he bought a cold drink and sat sipping it while his mind tried to fathom out what had just happened.

Was Brad running the company, or was Alyson trying to usurp his position and control things in the company? Either way, Fred decided that he was not going to follow it up. Instead, he would continue to enjoy his freedom and stay at home. The sun beat down on him as he sipped his cold drink and his mind then moved to the suggestion that Peter had made about holding a birthday party for him.

Fred took his mobile phone out of his pocket and dialed Peter's number.

"Hi Peter, it's Dad here."

"Hi Dad, what can I do for you at this time of the day?"

"Sorry to trouble you son, but you remember you mentioned a birthday party for your old man? Well, I've given it some thought and I think I'd like it, but will you do me a favor please?"

"Sure Dad, what's that?"

"Don't invite too many people!"

"Well, to be honest with you I had thought of a few of us, including the birthday boy going out to a show or something like that and then coming back to the house – your house I mean."

"But that's going to make it late, isn't it?" asked Fred.

"Hmm, maybe, but what I thought of was a night over the weekend and then when we come back to your house we could stay the night and party until we all dropped. How does that appeal to you?"

Fred grinned to himself as he immediately thought of the last time they had enjoyed a party at his house with all of Peter's friends.

"Does that mean you're inviting all your friends to the party?" asked Fred.

It was Peter's turn to grin to himself. His father knew him well, but they actually knew each other very well.

"I suppose you might say that," chuckled Peter over the phone.

"Fine, son, I don't mind. I'll leave it all to you to arrange."

"By the way, Dad, how did the interview go this morning?"

"Oh, don't even talk about that. I do not know who is running that place whether it is Brad or some woman from the finance department. She has no sense of humor and was not keen on me working part-time."

"But I thought you had spoken to Brad and it was all arranged."

"I did speak to him and it appeared from his point of view that everything would be fine. Well, that was until I met with Grizzabella!"

Peter roared with laughter on hearing Alyson's new name.

"So what are you going to do Dad? Are you going to tell Brad what happened?"

"No, son, I'm just going to leave it."

"But can I put Brad on the party list or should I leave him off?" enquired Peter.

"I have nothing against Brad, son. If you want to put him on, do so by all means, I really don't mind at all."

Peter made a mental note of that and then thought about Patrick and wondered if he might want to see Fred again, depending on where Patrick was now living. Should he ask his Dad if he was willing to see Patrick again or should he contact Patrick first to see if he was available and then spring it on his Dad as a surprise? It did not take Peter long to come to a decision – it would be a surprise. He would rather not mention it to his Dad just in case Patrick turned down the offer and then if he had mentioned it to his Dad, Fred might become disappointed.

Fred suddenly had a memory flash and asked, "Oh, by the way, and I almost forgot, how was the dinner, Peter?"

"Dinner, Dad?" questioned Peter, a little blankly.

"Yes, the nude dinner with your friends."

Realization struck in.

"Oh, yes sorry, I wasn't thinking properly. It was great fun, thanks."

"I hope nothing untoward happened. I mean, no private parts burnt as a result of falling food or such like things."

"Nothing like that, Dad. It all went well."

Fred thought that Peter was holding something back. He seemed reticent and not willing to talk about it, which was so unlike Peter. Peter had always been open with Fred to the extent that he even gave Fred every detail of his sexual activities. They had always been very open to each other since Peter was a small boy.

"Peter, is there something you're not telling me?"

"Not at all Dad. We had a wonderful evening."

Fred thought it wise not to pursue matters as it might upset Peter, but he still had this nagging feeling that Peter did know something more than he was letting on.

"Are you doing anything tonight, Peter? If not, would you like to come around maybe for a drink?"

"Keith and I were thinking of going to a movie and then heading to a bar for a drink or two."

"Fine, fine! Maybe another night then," said Fred, a little subdued at the rejection of his invitation. This was now the second rejection he had received in one day! He switched off his mobile phone.

Fred was, for the first time, beginning to feel that those around him might be alienating themselves from him and he wondered if this was because of his age. Is this what happened to all old people, or people reaching, what might be regarded, as old age? He knew that he had endured rejection previously, so he understood that it was merely a part of life, but it seemed odd to receive two rejections in one day. He tried to shake it from his mind and focus on something else.

He moved out of the sunshine and went into his bedroom, pulled on a Speedo and decided to spend some time out by the swimming pool, tanning and swimming and just having time to himself. He grabbed a towel and a book to read and headed out to the pool, taking his mobile phone with him, just in case there were any calls for him.

Outside the sun blazed down and without a slight breeze, the air was hot and almost clammy. He threw down the towel on a pool lounger and lay down to absorb the sun's rays. He poured some tanning oil over his chest and massaged it into his body. As he did so, and his hands slid over the curvature of his pectoral muscles, he realised that he still had a very well defined body and that age really had nothing to do with his present day. Yes, he still was fit and healthy, and yes, he still had a good body, but why were people now looking differently at him, he wondered.

Fred lay on the lounger feeling the sun soak into his body and as it soaked in, so he began to doze. His mind drifted to thinking of how he and Patrick had first met, and how he felt about Patrick. As his mind drifted, so memories flooded in and he felt himself becoming aroused, thinking of Patrick. He suddenly opened his eyes and looked down at the massive bulge that had developed in his Speedo. He smiled to himself, ran a hand over it and had very happy thoughts. He then rose from the lounger and dived into the cool water, hoping that its coolness might get the massive bulge to subside. As he swam to the other side of the pool, he heard a voice coming from behind him.

"Hi Fred. I rang the doorbell but there was no answer. I saw that your car was here so I tried the front door handle and made my way in," said Brad.

Fred was somewhat surprised by Brad's appearance, but pulled himself from the pool, water dripping everywhere and walked over to Brad, the bulge still evident. Brad's eyes caught site of the massive bulge and a smile enveloped his face.

"Sorry, was I interrupting something?" questioned Brad.

"No, not at all. Why?"

"Well …" said Brad, pointing to Fred's excited appearance.

Fred laughed heartily.

"Oh that! I was just lying here dreaming."

"Well I hope, that he was nice," replied Brad.

"Oh yes, very nice," grinned Fred, flinging himself back onto his pool lounger while Brad pulled up another lounger to sit next to Fred.

"Anyone I know?" asked Brad, trying or hoping to get Fred to divulge who had been responsible for this excitement.

"Mm! I think you do," was all that Fred was prepared to say.

"So you're not going to tell me!"

Fred merely shook his head and grinned, blushing at the same time. So what brings you here?" queried Fred, thinking that he might know why Brad was there.

"Fred, I was wondering why you decided not to join us at the company as I thought you wanted to have a part-time job."

"Yes I do, but I got the feeling that there actually wasn't anything there for me."

Brad looked somewhat puzzled.

"I don't understand," said Brad.

"Well, I spoke to Alyson and she seemed to think that I wouldn't fit in there and there wasn't anything on a part-time basis."

"Oh, you don't have to say anything more, Fred."

"I don't understand."

"You see, I am in partnership in the business with Alyson's husband, and I have noticed over time how she tries to control who joins the company and what goes on there. It's not the first time that she's jeopardized something that I had planned or undermined some idea of mine."

"Hey, it's not a problem, Brad. I accept her decision."

"Well, I don't," replied Brad. "I'll tell you what, I have another option for you if you would be interested. What I also do is buy up properties, redo them, and then sell them. What I would like is someone to oversee the interior decor and the refurbishing of the houses or apartments. Would you be interested in that, Fred?"

"Do you mean that?"

"Yes, absolutely. You see, I have to leave the office so often to supervise the guys and it upsets my day sometimes. So to have someone I can trust watching over the guys and helping with the decor would make my life a great deal easier, and looking at the way you have decorated your homes, both the old one and this one, impresses me."

Fred broke into a broad smile at the offer.

"I would love to do that, Brad. Wow! That sounds so exciting." Fred laughed heartily. "I could even hug you and give you a kiss."

"So, what's stopping you?" enquired Brad, with a naughty glint in his eyes.

Fred rose from the lounger and crossed over to Brad where he threw his arms around him and pulled him close to his chest. He then planted a kiss on Brad's lips. The two men stood hugging and kissing for some time and Brad was obviously enjoying the moment, as he did not try to pull away from Fred's clutches. Brad could feel the heavy bulge from Fred's Speedo pressed up against his stomach and to him it felt good, and he began to get aroused by their physical contact.

Eventually, Fred's lips broke free from Brad's.

"Thank you Brad, you have really made my day for me."

"I'm glad about that and I'm glad that I was able to sort out the problem caused by Alyson," said Brad, holding Fred tightly to him.

Fred gave him another kiss and they remained locked in each other's arms. What was going through Brad or Fred's heads was unknown to either of them, but they were happy together.

"Wow!" said Fred, eventually breaking free from Brad's embrace and lying down on the lounger once more. "When can I start?"

"Tomorrow, if you like," replied Brad.

Fred noticed his engorged bulge in his Speedo and added, "You see what you did to me?"

"Hey, getting that involves two people so don't put all the blame on me," laughed Brad as he settled on the lounger next to Fred.

"You know what, I would actually prefer the position you have just offered me than working in an office all day, especially with that woman Alyson."

"Well, I think that we're going to get on just fine," said Brad, fiddling with the crotch of his jeans.

"You have a problem there, Brad?" asked Fred, grinning at his new boss.

"Sort of, but it can be handled, thanks," replied Brad.

"Hey, I've been so rude and concerned about my own issues, I forgot to offer you something to drink. Can I get you anything, Brad?"

"No thanks, it's fine. However, I think I should be making my way home as I only wanted to find out what had happened today and why you weren't joining us."

"Hey listen, Brad, I want to ask you if you'd like to come around for my birthday? Peter is supposed to be arranging something over a weekend so everyone can stay over if they want to."

"When is your birthday, Fred?"

"It's actually next Wednesday, so I'm presuming that Peter is looking at either the Friday night or Saturday next week. Would either of those days suit you?"

"I'll tell you what, in theory it's going to be fine, but let me check my diary and get back to you."

"No problem, but I will tell Peter that I have already spoken to you so he doesn't have to contact you, except to confirm the date and time. He said something about going to a show and then coming back to the house for the rest of the evening. I have no actual idea as to the show or even who he's planning on inviting, but knowing him, I'm sure it will be fun."

"Fred, I'll try to make sure that I'm here that night. Should I contact Peter or you?"

"I think you'd better contact Peter as if he's thinking of a show, he'd have to book tickets for it and he would have to know numbers then."

Brad leaned down to give Fred another hug while he lay on the pool lounger and at the same time, planted a kiss on Fred's lips.

"Bye, sexy man, I'll send one of my guys around to pick you up tomorrow and take you to the apartment that they are busy working on," quipped Brad as he stood up.

"Thanks Brad, I'll be ready for them. Bye sexy boss," retorted Fred, with a gleam in his eyes. "Do you want me to show you out or are you fine seeing yourself out?"

"I think I can manage as I did see myself in when I arrived," responded Brad, giving a wave of the hand and departing through the house.

Actually, he did not seem such a bad person after all, thought Fred. Maybe over the years, Brad had changed for the better. As Fred lay basking in the sun, his mind went back to the last time that Brad had stayed over at the house when Peter had invited a number of his friends, and the trouble that Brad had caused by flirting with virtually every man in the house. Was Brad now doing the same thing again, but this time flirting with Fred? Alternatively, was Fred just imagining things, after all he was a friendly guy and he had just given Fred a part-time job, and a good one at that.

A sense of excitement filled Fred as he thought of how he could utilize his artistic abilities to decorate developments that Brad was upgrading in order to resell. He closed his eyes and visualized himself in charge, creating beauty within the homes of future buyers. In his mind's eye, he could see the workers hurrying from room to room to ready the property for Brad to resell it. Then he visualized the last-minute preparations as the deadline draws ever closer and how proud he felt when the deal was closed and the new owner walked into the apartment or house and saw what he and the workers had done.

The sun made Fred doze off for a while and when he awoke, he felt a little cold as he was now lying in shade. He raised himself from the pool lounger and made his way indoors to put on some clothes and have something to drink.

CHAPTER 5

Just as Brad had promised, Fred heard the roar of a vehicle's engine outside the front entrance to his house. He peered through the hall window and saw a rather ramshackle truck outside. He opened the front door and yelled to the driver.

"Are you the guy from Brad to pick me up?"

"Yes, sir," came a burly voice.

"I wasn't expecting you so early. Why not switch off and come in for some coffee while I get ready?" called Fred.

The engine to the noisy vehicle was cut, the driver's door opened and a large, burly man exited from it. He strode towards Fred, arm outstretched.

"Don, at your service, Sir," he said, taking Fred's hand and shaking it with manly force.

"Hi, I'm Fred. Come in and make yourself at home."

Fred closed the front door and led Don into the lounge.

"Coffee, Don?"

"Thanks Fred. Milk and two sugars please."

Don must have been about six foot tall, looking about thirty-eight years old and appeared to be all muscle. Fred could see how the biceps fought hard with the sleeves of Don's T-shirt, stretching them to their limits. Don's right arm was covered in an ornate tattoo, which resembled something likely to be found in Samoa or Fiji. The stretch of fabric clearly outlined Don's chest. It almost looked like Don had owned his T-shirt from the days when he was a size small and should now be wearing something in the extra-large size range. As Fred looked at the taut material across Don's chest, he was sure that he noticed the two nipples had something either attached to them or running through them. Don noticed how Fred had focused on his nipples, so he thought it might make Fred feel more relaxed by knowing that his nipples were pierced.

"Isn't that painful, Don?" asked Fred, genuinely intrigued.

"I suppose you might say it was a bit sore when it was being done, but you know they say, "no beauty without pain!" and I was prepared to endure any pain."

Fred laughed nervously and added, "Dare I ask if there are any more piercings?"

Don also added his laughter.

"Oh yes, just one more," replied Don, but did not elaborate.

Fred was tempted to ask, but chose not to and instead let Don offer an answer if he so wished, which he did not.

"I have been thinking of getting them pierced thicker," continued Don, this time running his fingers over both nipples as he spoke.

"Thicker!" replied Fred. "How do you mean?"

"Well at the moment all my piercings have thin bars through them, but I want them to have thicker bars through them – it makes for greater sensation," answered Don, proudly.

Fred's imagination flashed as he tried to visualize the metal bars running through Don's nipples and wherever else the other piercing was. He then excused himself to make the coffee, and hurried through to the kitchen.

"Make yourself at home, Don," shouted Fred from the kitchen.

While Fred made the coffee, he thought that Don looked somewhat familiar but couldn't place him. Maybe it was just one of those faces that you see in a crowd, or that you focus so much on the well-built torso that you forget the face and they all end up looking the same. The coffee was made and brought in to Don, while Fred hurried off to his bedroom to get changed.

"Do you live alone?" shouted Don from the lounge.

"Yes," came the reply

"Isn't it lonely," shouted Don, sipping his coffee.

"Yeah, I suppose sometimes it is," replied Fred, entering the lounge zipping up his jeans and then buttoning up his shirt and tucking it into his jeans. "I think I've got used to it by now, but it's not so lonely as my son often visits."

"Oh, were you married?"

"Divorced," answered Fred.

"So, no one in your life now?"

"At the moment I'm single and available," laughed Fred.

Don slurped his coffee now in an effort to get it down as quickly as he could so they could set off to work.

"What about you, Don? Are you married?"

"No, also single and I suppose available too," he laughed, realizing that he had copied Fred.

"Not even a girlfriend?" asked Fred.

"I did have, but I dumped her," said Don with a sense of achievement in his voice.

Fred wondered why it was that men always wanted to sound as though they had the upper hand when there was a break up between couples. He wondered if he had said that he divorced his wife instead of her divorcing him. Maybe he had when they first split up, but now he was quite happy to admit that she had divorced him

"Are you ready, Fred?"

"Yes, whenever you are."

Don gulped down the last dregs of coffee, rose from the chair he had been sitting in and the two men left the house.

Once they had climbed into the noisy truck, and started on their journey, Fred glance across to Don and wondered how the large man had managed to squeeze himself into his tight jeans, let alone his T-shirt. He had not asked Don what his function in the job was, but he assumed that he must be a builder with all his muscles.

"How many guys are we working with, Don?"

"Counting you Fred, three. You, me and Paul."

"What do you and Paul actually do when you're on the building or construction site?"

"I'm usually the builder and Paul's the electrician cum plumber."

"So I presume then that I am the interior decorator?" chuckled Fred. "But tell me, what happens to you two guys when there isn't any actual building or plumbing to be done?"

Don laughed as he answered.

"We do anything, and I mean anything!"

Fred"s mind flew into turmoil as he tried to determine what Don meant by "anything". Did this mean that they could paint, hang pictures and curtaining, arrange flowers, mop the floors or do anything that they were asked to do?

"So what's Paul like?" asked Fred, trying to forget about the "other" tasks that Don and Paul might do.

"He's not a bad guy... very friendly... pretty fit... I don't know, just a good guy, I suppose."

This did not give Fred too much information about Paul, but he knew that he would soon meet Paul and draw his own conclusion as to what his new work mates were like. The truck trundled along the road, belching clouds of exhaust fumes every so often and rattling like it was about to fall to pieces, but at no time did Don ever consider reducing the speed.

They finally drew up outside a block of apartments that were in the process of being constructed.

"This is it, Fred. Don't worry, we're not working on all of these. Brad has bought one of the apartments and it has to be decorated and finished off. It's going to be the show apartment for the building," said Don, climbing out of the truck and slamming the driver's door shut.

Fred followed suit and stood staring up at the four-storey building.

"We're on the top floor, Fred. Come on, mate."

Don led and both he and Fred made their way up to the top floor, walked along a long corridor and eventually came to number one, situated on the corner of the top floor. Don opened the front door and went in, followed closely by Fred.

"You here, Paul?" shouted Don.

"In the main bedroom," came a reply.

Don led the way to the main bedroom with Fred following and admiring what he saw. As Fred walked through the apartment, he was struck by the view from the lounge windows, which opened out onto a large balcony. Even though it was only on the fourth floor, the building was built on a hill overlooking the city, giving a perfect view of the whole city and its surrounding areas. All the furnishings were placed in the center of the lounge area and Fred realised that his job would be to organize the positioning of this furniture. As they entered the main bedroom, Fred caught sight of someone, whom he presumed to be Paul.

"Hi Paul," said Don, as he entered the room. "Let me introduce you to our new partner. This is Fred and he's going to be sorting out the decor for us."

Paul was a tall, slim twenty-something young man with a shock of blonde hair that looked as if he had dyed it rather than it being natural blonde. In fact, the more Fred looked at the color of Paul's hair, the more he began to think of a surfer.

"Hi Paul, pleased to meet you," said Fred shaking hands with Paul.

"Same here, Fred. So you're the guy who's going to do the furniture moving," said Paul, grinning broadly.

"I suppose if you put it that way, yes," replied Fred.

"Have you finished with the re-wiring, Paul?" enquired Don, looking around the room.

"All complete. It's just for Fred to move the furniture in here and fix up the room then this one will be finished," answered Paul.

Don crossed over to the light switch near the bedroom door and switched it on. The concealed lighting illuminated the room.

"Not bad, buddy," said Don noticing the lighting coming from artificial panels against the wall where the headboard of the master bed would be placed. "Obviously, Fred, this is where the king sized bed has to be placed."

Fred nodded his head in acknowledgement.

"Are you happy with that, Don?" enquired Paul.

"Absolutely! I think that Fred can start moving furniture into this room while we sort out the bathroom. Is that okay with you, Fred?" asked Don. "Paul, you come with me."

Fred again nodded that he knew what he had to do and started looking around the room to decide where to place everything. He knew now where the master bed had to be placed and it was just a matter of selecting artworks, mirrors and other pieces of furniture. Don and Paul left the bedroom and made their way to the bathroom, to complete whatever needed to be done.

Fred started by moving the king-size bed into place, then looking at where the remaining space was so he could position the dressing table, easy chairs and hang curtains and pictures. He had noticed that the general color scheme of the curtains and fittings consisted of varying shades of blue. He then moved in the dressing table, which took some effort on his own, but he was strong and managed it quite easily.

Things were coming together quite quickly in the main bedroom and Fred was enjoying himself as he positioned paintings and mirrors, but it took some time to hang the curtains, as he did not have a stepladder in order to reach the curtain rail.

Fred decided to go and look for Paul or Don. He wandered towards the bathroom where the other two men had said they would be working. As Fred neared the bathroom door, he heard some noises, but not of men talking. He hesitated outside of the bathroom door and listened intently. The noises sounded familiar. He himself had made those noises and had heard others making them as well. It was of two people kissing and obviously breathing heavily and groaning. He was tempted to open the door to see what was happening but then he thought how embarrassing it might be, if in fact Paul and Don were kissing or doing something more than just kissing. He stood there waiting to hear if there might be a pause when he could call out or knock on the door, allowing them time to get themselves disentangled, should that be the case. The noises went on for what seemed an eternity and this meant that Fred's work was being delayed, so he decided to knock on the bathroom door.

"Yes!" came Don's voice.

"Sorry to worry you, but I need a stepladder in order to hang the curtains," replied Fred.

The bathroom door opened and Don appeared, and Fred could see Don's T-shirt lying on the bathroom floor. The half-naked Don came out of the bathroom and took Fred into the kitchen to get the stepladder.

"I'm sorry if I disturbed you," said Fred.

Don blushed slightly.

"No problem, Fred," said the burly Don, smiling coyly, which was something that Fred did not expect Don to be able to do. "If you need help in hanging them, give us a shout and one of us will come and help you."

"Thanks Don," said Fred, smiling knowingly.

As Fred walked back to the main bedroom and passed the bathroom, he noticed that Paul was also shirtless and he could see the trim, yet athletic build of the young man.

When Fred got back to the bedroom, he wondered if Don and Paul were lovers. On the other hand, he wondered whether it was just a moment of passion that was taking place between them.

The curtains went up easily and when Fred dismounted the stepladder and stood back, he admired his work and thought that the bedroom looked both elegant and restful. He stepped out of the bedroom and instead of going to the bathroom, in case Don and Paul were busy doing something other than working on the bathroom fittings, he shouted to them.

"Hey guys! Do you want to come and see the main bedroom?"

"Sure!" came the reply from Don.

When Paul and Don came out of the bathroom, both had their shirts back on, but Fred chose not to say anything.

"Let's see what you've done, mate," said Don, casually.

All three made their way into the main bedroom and both Paul and Don were impressed by what they saw.

"That looks pretty hot," said Paul as he wandered around the bedroom.

"It looks cool and sexy," commented Don. "You did a pretty good job and I think that Brad will be very pleased with this, Fred. Well done," said Don, taking Fred's hand and shaking it.

Fred felt elated and felt that he had pleased Don, who seemed the senior in the work environment, so it made Fred feel that the other two had accepted him.

"You're part of the team now, Fred," said Paul, patting Fred on the back.

Fred smiled and then gave a little laugh as he was not quite sure what Paul really meant by being part of the team. Don and Paul eyed the large king-size bed and wondered if, when Fred was not around whether they would try out the mattress!

"Listen Fred, we don't normally duck out for lunch, so you're welcome to share lunch with us," said Don, feeling more accommodating towards Fred. "We usually share whatever we have."

"That's fine with me," replied Fred, "but I didn't bring any lunch to share with you guys."

"Not a problem, Fred. We have enough for the three of us," added Paul, producing a large take out box of Chinese noodles.

The three men went into the kitchen, found some paper plates and shared out the food of Chinese noodles, sandwiches and coffee from a flask. Fred was touched by their hospitality and friendship as well as their willingness to accept him into their world. After all, Fred knew that he was so many years older than they were but they had not worried about his age. As they sat eating their lunch and conversing in a general chitchat, Fred noticed that there was a definite bond between Don and Paul. He also remembered that Don had said he had neither a wife nor a girlfriend, so maybe he and Paul were lovers, not that this concerned him. After all, he was gay and so was his son and he had enjoyed a good relationship with Patrick at one time.

With lunch over, it was back to work and this time Fred went into the lounge to try and sort out some of the mess that the cluttered furniture was making.

"Who selected all the furnishings?" asked Fred as he entered the lounge with Don and Paul.

"Brad did," answered Don. "However, now that you are working for him, that will be one of your tasks to do in future."

Fred liked the idea of visiting stores and purchasing fittings and furnishing.

"I thought of trying to get the lounge sorted out so it will give you guys more space instead of having to juggle yourselves around all this clutter," said Fred.

"Good idea," replied Don. "Paul and I can then go into the second bedroom and get those lighting fixtures sorted out."

The two "lovers" went off to the second bedroom, while Fred began to busy himself, sorting and arranging the furniture in the lounge. It did not take Fred long to have the lounge looking elegant and orderly. He stood back and admired his work, feeling proud of his achievement. This time, he shouted to Don and Paul to come and approve of his handiwork, rather than go into the bedroom in case they were busy with each other again.

The two men entered the clean, well laid out lounge and both smiled broadly.

"What a difference some order makes." commented Paul, wandering around the lounge and looking carefully as to where each piece of furniture had been placed in relation to the other pieces.

"I'm really impressed, Fred," said Don, standing next to him and placing a muscular arm around Fred's shoulders. "I honestly think that Brad will like this. It looks clean and well planned. There's ample walking space between the pieces and there's still plenty of room to add extra items should he wish to do so."

Fred felt elated by the response from both Don and Paul and was proud of himself knowing that he could do the things that he had often dreamed of doing.

"I reckon you can have a break Fred, while Paul and I finish in the second bedroom, then we'll take you back home," said Don.

Fred sat himself down on the comfortable sofa to wait for the others to finish their work, and to sit back and view his interior decor skills. As he sat there he could hear Paul and Don chatting to each other in the second bedroom, but after a while he realised that it had become quiet. He wondered if the two men were still working or whether they were taking a break. He rose and quietly made his way towards the second bedroom. The bedroom door was partly closed, but he was able to see through the doorjamb that both men were naked and lying on the floor in the room. He stood transfixed as he watched Paul kneeling between Don's muscular legs. He could see Paul bent over Don's erect penis and Paul's head was rising and falling above the older man. He then heard Don whisper something to Paul, who stopped what he was doing, adjusted his position and began to lower his young ass onto the thick, long penis that awaited him. Fred heard both men sigh loudly as Paul sank lower onto Don's manhood and then they both started thrusting and pushing. Fred watched for a moment, felt his own arousal forming and then headed back to the lounge to await Don and Paul's arrival.

When the two men came back into the lounge, they both looked flush, but both seemed relaxed and content. Fred never mentioned a word of what he had seen.

"Sorry we took so long, Fred..."

"... not a problem Don," answered Fred hurriedly, as he did not want to hear an explanation, not that he disapproved of what either man had been doing. In fact, he knew that he was envious that he did not have someone with whom he could share his love.

The three of them climbed into the truck, Don driving while Paul sat next to Don and Fred seated against the passenger door, and headed off to Fred's house to drop him off. As they drove along, Fred could feel the body warmth emanating from Paul and it made him feel aroused by the young man's physical proximity, but he did nothing to encourage his younger friend.

When they arrived at Fred's house, he invited the men in for a drink but they turned down the offer and drove off, leaving Fred to think on his first day of work.

CHAPTER 6

The wind howled as it swept across the open sea towards the land, cutting through electrical wires and trees, causing street signs to swing wildly, litter to fly in all directions and for Fred to remain snuggled up in bed. It was not that he was ill, not that he was with someone, but when he awoke early in the morning and heard the wind howling, he decided that bed was the best place. He knew that he did not have to work, as Don and Paul were working on another project for Brad, which did not entail Fred having to do any decor. He snuggled under the duvet and thought, "this is the time when one needs someone to share the bed and make love." Alas, now, there was no one for him so he just closed his eyes and tried to doze off to sleep again.

A loud ringing awoke him. He took a moment to come back to the reality of everyday life. It was his mobile phone ringing. He stretched across from the bed to the side table on which the phone lay. He picked it up and in a sleepy voice, answered the call.

"Hi, Fred speaking," came the croaky voice.

"Hey! Are you sick, old man?" came the voice at the other end of the phone.

"Who's that?" asked the dream-like Fred.

"It's Brad. Have you just woken up?"

"Mm," came the grunt. "Sorry Brad, what can I do for you?"

"I just wanted to thank you for what you've done so far for the apartment of mine. Don told me how you had arranged everything to his liking and if it pleases him, then I know it will please me."

"Oh, thanks Brad," replied Fred, groggily.

"He said that he was able to leave you on your own and you were able to sort things out. That is what I wanted and you produced the goods. Thanks buddy. I hope that neither he nor Paul was any trouble and they were able to help you if you needed it."

Fred was unsure as to what Brad meant by the two men being any trouble, but he was not about to mention the good time that Paul and Don had in the apartment.

"They were no problem, Brad. They just got on and did their work while I did mine."

"I'm glad to hear that. I've had them working for me for about a year now and I think they seem to work well together," continued Brad.

A wry smile crossed Fred's face on hearing Brad's opinion of Don and Paul. He wondered if Brad had any idea as to the romance between the two men taking place, but it was not for him to mention it nor was he going to blow Don and Paul's cover, so to speak.

"You're right Brad, they do work well together," replied Fred, allowing a little chuckle to break free, as he visualized their bedroom sex all over again.

"Listen, Fred, I have spoken to Peter and told him that I had spoken to you and would be attending your birthday party, but I was unsure if I would attend the show beforehand."

"That's not a problem, Brad. If you can make it to the party, that will be great. If you can make it to the show as well, that will be even better."

"Have you any idea what show Peter has in mind?" asked Brad.

"I really have no idea as he hasn't mentioned anything to me – it's all being kept secret," laughed Fred.

"Well, listen, I'll let you know when Don will be picking you up again, and keep up the good work, Fred."

"Thanks Brad, and have a great day yourself."

"Cheers, Fred."

Fred switched off his mobile phone, replaced it on the bedside table and snuggled under the duvet again, and dozed off to sleep.

Sleep came quickly to Fred. His mind began to drift into an almost somnambulistic state, except he was not sleepwalking, but rather his mind went on a journey. He sank slowly into a dream world.

Fred saw himself lying on a desolate beach. It was a calm, sunny day with no evident breath of air. The gentle ebb and flow of the sea was the only sound that penetrated his brain. He lay with his eyes closed and merely absorbed the warmth of the sun. As he lay there, the lull of the waves seemed to hypnotize him in his dream-like state. The warmth continued for some time until he began to feel a lack of warmth on his face – it was as if a cloud had obliterated the sun. He gingerly opened his eyes to see what was blocking the sun's rays. The silhouette of someone stood above him. He instinctively blinked as if to clear his eyesight, but when he thought he had adjusted his eye line, he could see that the silhouette remained there. A voice, that sounded distant, called his name.

"Fred!" sounded the voice.

"Yes," answered Fred in a dream-like hollowness.

"What is the one wish that you have?"

Fred did not understand the relevance of such a question and blinked again, unsure if there was an actual person standing there speaking to him or not.

"I have no wish," murmured Fred.

"What is the one thing you desire the most?" asked the voice.

Fred remained lying flat on his back on the sand, looking up at the silhouette. He was unable to make out the finer details of the silhouette, but could ascertain that the being was tall and slim.

"Who are you?" enquired Fred.

"I am part of your mind, Fred," came the reply.

"I don't understand."

"Don't let your mind confuse you, Fred. I represent your inner soul. I am the one thing missing in your life."

"The one thing missing in my life", thought Fred.

"Nothing is missing in my life," retorted Fred. "I'm happy with everything I have."

"What are your life ambitions?"

"I have done everything that I have wanted to do, so I have no life ambitions left," replied Fred.

"What of memories, Fred?"

"What do you mean?"

"Think, Fred."

Fred was becoming frustrated yet felt he was unable to raise himself up on an elbow to get a better view of the silhouette. It felt as if he had been pinned to the sand, and unable to move.

"You have memories of which I am but one."

"Then who are you?" said Fred, in a desperate tone.

"Think Fred. Life is not always so easy that you are merely given the answers. Life is so you can think and develop your thoughts, and not expect them to be handed to you so easily. Go back in your thoughts, Fred, and think what your inner soul desired so much."

Fred lay there in his dream-like state, thinking while the silhouette remained shading his face. After a while, Fred began to toss his head from left to right as if shaking his head.

"I cannot think of anything," cried Fred in sheer desperation.

"Think of me," said the silhouette, as it began to move slightly allowing the sun's rays to fall back onto Fred's face.

"But who are you?" Fred once again cried out.

In crying out, he suddenly woke himself and his eyes opened wide as if in shock. Fred sat up erect in bed and looked around him. Yes, he was still in bed and there was no sand around him. It must have been a dream, but what did it mean, and who was the silhouette that he had seen? Fred sat up in bed for a moment, and then he threw back the duvet and slid from the bed. He padded his way into his en suite bathroom and splashed his face with cold water, in order to waken himself properly. He then opened the shower door, switched on the shower, stepped out of his sleep shorts and stepped into the shower. He let the warm water splash over his athletic body and he stood there, head thrown back enjoying the feel of the water as it cascaded down his chest and back and on down his legs. As he stood there letting the water caress his body, he heard his mobile phone ring. He thought of rushing out of the shower to answer the phone, but something made him stay where he was. The phone stopped ringing and then there soon followed a "beep" indicating there was a message for him.

Fred switched off the faucet, stepped out of the shower and grabbed a towel. He began to dry himself when his mobile phone rang once more. This time he moved to the phone and switched it on.

"Hello, Fred speaking."

"Hi Dad, where were you? I just phoned you and it just rang and rang."

"I was in the shower Peter. Why, what's the matter?"

"Nothing serious, but I wanted to know if you had any numbers for me about how many people you have invited to your party as I was going to book tickets for the show."

"I thought you were organizing everything, son."

"Yes, I am but I know you often invite your own friends so I need to know if any of them are coming to the show."

"I know that Brad won't be attending and I haven't invited any others yet so I would suggest that you book for you, Keith and me, and whoever else you've invited that will be attending. I get the feeling that some will only arrive for the party and not the show."

"That's the impression I've also got, so I'll go ahead and book for three of us."

"Great, Peter. Just as a matter of interest, what show are you planning on taking us to?"

"There's a new play that's just opened called "Stark Raving Naked". I thought we might like to have a laugh."

"With a title like, that it could only be a comedy. Any idea what it's about?"

"I believe it's a gay play about relationships," answered Peter.

"That should be interesting," replied Fred, thinking that they might all benefit from an understanding of relationships, but not saying such to Peter. "What time does it start and have you decided whether we're having the party on Friday or Saturday night?"

"I thought we'd have the party on Saturday night so everyone who wants to can stay over and leave on the Sunday. I'm booking for the early show on Saturday, at 6pm."

"Sounds fine to me, son. Are you two guys going to meet me there or are we going to go in one car?"

"Do you think you could pick Keith and I up and then we can come back to your place? It just means that you would have to take us home on Sunday, if that's fine with you?"

"I don't have a problem with that, provided you and Keith are happy with the plan."

"Look, I'll speak to Keith and see what he says and then get back to you."

"Sounds great, Peter, and thanks for organizing all this."

"My pleasure, Dad."

"Now do you think I can get dressed, as I'm standing here naked and getting cold?"

"Oops, sorry Dad. Yeah, you'd better get dressed before some hot man comes and knocks on your door, like the pizza delivery man!"

Peter roared with laughter as he thought back to the evening that the pizza delivery man stood gaping at Fred's crotch.

"What are you laughing at, Peter?" asked Fred.

"Just rekindling that night, that's all. Now get dressed Dad. I will be in touch. Cheers, Dad."

"Bye, son," said Fred, smiling to himself and switching off his mobile phone.

Fred dried himself thoroughly, pulled on a pair of briefs and shorts, a T-shirt and his sneakers, then wandered out into his lounge. The level of the wind's intensity had reduced considerably and the howling through the electric wires and trees had diminished. The clouds had begun to clear and the sun was creeping through those clouds that were still hovering above. Fred's mind went back to his dream that he'd had early that morning. He wondered if it had been some sort of message of something about to happen, or whether it was merely his subconscious working overtime.

The front door bell rang three times, so Fred wandered through form the lounge to see who was at the door. He opened the door and there stood Don.

"Hi Don, what are you doing here. I'm not supposed to be working today."

"Hi Fred. I know that you're not supposed to be at work today, but I was wondering if you could help me."

"Why, where's Paul?"

"He's unable to help today as he's not feeling so well. It means that I'm on my own and I wondered if you wouldn't mind just assisting me for a couple of hours."

"Come in, Don, and let me put some other clothes on."

"No need, Fred. You can come as you are. It's mainly to hold things or get things for me. All the manual labor will be done by me."

"Are you sure?"

"Absolutely."

"Well, if you are sure. Let me just lock up and then we can get on our way."

Fred grabbed a couple of snacks for both of them and some bottles

of water, and then locked up the house. They drove to the complex that
Fred had worked on, Don unlocked the apartment door, and they went in.

"I need to finish some work in the kitchen, Fred, so if you wouldn't
mind helping me there, I'd appreciate that. It shouldn't take us too long."

"Hey! You just tell me what you want done and I'll do it," said
Fred, placing the bottles of water and the snacks on the kitchen counter.
"So what's first?"

"I need to fix the light shades to the lights and wire the stove to
begin with and then sort out a couple of storage cupboards."

"That sounds pretty easy," responded Fred. "So what must I do?"

"The shades are in the second bedroom on the floor. If you can
bring those to me, that would be great. While you get those, I'll start on
the wiring of the stove."

Fred made his way to the second bedroom to collect the kitchen
shades. As he entered the room, he remembered the sight he had seen
through the doorjamb. He could see the spot where Paul and Don had
been lying on the floor and he could remember how Don was enjoying
the pleasure of pleasing young Paul. He found the light shades but did
not leave the room. He wondered how Paul must have felt as Don took
advantage of him and both men enjoyed their sexual pleasure. This was
something that Fred was missing in his life. He wondered if that was the
message or idea, to which the dream was referring.

"Can you find them?" shouted Don.

"Yes, I've got them," came back the call from the bedroom.

Fred hurried back to the kitchen and duly handed the light shades
to Don.

"Thanks buddy," said Don, taking them from Fred and placing
them on the kitchen counter while he finished wiring the stove.

As Fred stood watching Don at work, he decided to invite Don to
his birthday party.

"Hey, Don, I was wondering if you would like to come to my
birthday party on Saturday night. When I say you, I mean you and a

partner. My son's organizing a few friends around as he feels the old man needs a birthday party, but I think in actual fact he's looking for an excuse to have a party of his own."

"Gee, thanks Fred, that sounds great. I would like that. Would you mind if I brought Paul along as you know him and we do work together?"

Fred smiled broadly. He felt that this clearly indicated that Don and Paul must be in some sort of relationship and he was happy to have both men at the party.

"That would be my pleasure. Both of you come. Oh, and remember it's casual, so no formality in dress."

"What time, Fred?"

"I would say any time after about 8:30pm as my son has arranged for me to go and see a six o'clock show with him and his partner before the party. The idea is for those who want, to stay overnight at my place. We'll just sleep wherever we fall, I should imagine," laughed Fred.

"Now that sounds like a party to me," replied Don, finishing off the wiring for the stove. "How many people are you expecting?"

Again Fred laughed. "I have no idea as my son is supposed to be organizing everything. All I know is that Brad will be there along with you and Paul. So with me, my son and his partner, that makes six, but I'm sure that he'll invite others."

"I like that," said Don, busying himself in the kitchen.

"Tell me, Don, do you understand dreams?" asked Fred, hesitantly.

Don laughed and added, "I used to read about it many years ago. Why, have you been having dreams?"

"I had one this morning and I've been trying to fathom it out ever since."

"What was it about?" asked Don, adjusting one of the light shades.

"Well the thing was set on a desolate beach and there was a silhouette standing over me, blocking out the sun," replied Fred.

"I think the desolate beach has something to do with something missing from your life. Sand is often considered as being soft so it could mean that things are getting away from you. As for the silhouette, it could represent a shadow over you. In other words something missing in your life or a stranger coming into your life, but I'm no expert."

"I suppose it might make sense, Don. After all, I am turning sixty-five so maybe things are disappearing in my life. As for the stranger, the only new people to come into my life are you and Paul."

Don roared with laughter.

"Maybe, but I don't think it was that," said Don, still chuckling heartily.

"Why not? No one else has come into my life lately, other than you and Paul."

"Anything else in the dream?" asked Don.

"No, other than the silhouette asking "what is the one thing you desire most?" and I can't think of the relevance of that."

"Well, maybe the one thing that you desire most is companionship and that is where the stranger coming into your life comes into play," suggested Don.

Now it was Fred's turn to laugh in disbelief.

"I'm not so sure about that, Don."

"Don't ever doubt the subconscious, Fred. It can become a source of vital information for you."

Fred listened to Don carefully. He wondered where this burly man gained all this insight.

"Where does all this come from Don?" asked Fred, somewhat puzzled.

"I suppose you think me as being all muscle and no brain, hey? Well I once used to be a teacher but knew that I could make more money as a handyman than what the education department paid me, so I resigned and joined the building sector."

Fred was truly amazed by this revelation and immediately his estimation of Don skyrocketed.

"Great, that's the last light shade fitted," said Don relieved and happy to have the job completed. "Now, can I take you home?"

"Is that it?" enquired Fred, surprised how little work he was required to do.

"I'm sorry that I brought you out Fred, but I didn't know what assistance I would need, but I'm grateful to you."

"Hey, it's my pleasure, Don. After all, I think I got to the bottom of my dream, thanks to you."

Both men laughed together as Don began to put away his tools and equipment. When Don had finished, he put an arm around Fred's shoulder and pulled him closer.

"You really are part of our team," said Don, "and I'm proud to know you and work with you."

Fred wondered if this was a genuine touch of affection, or was Don coming onto him in some sort of sexual way? Either way, Fred enjoyed the manly affection that Don was showing him. He could feel the strong man's arms embracing him and a warm fuzzy feeling came over Fred. He had not been hugged like this for some time. In fact, Patrick was the last man to have done this to him. Fred felt the urge to put his arms around Don and hug him back, but was unsure as to Don's feelings about that. Don's grasp on Fred tightened and instinctively Fred responded by hugging Don back. The two men stood face to face, chest-to-chest and crotch to crotch, hugging. Fred could feel the start of an arousal in his shorts, and at the same time, he could feel something hard pressing up against his crotch. Fred never tried to break free and enjoyed the moment.

Don could feel Fred's arousal against him and he smiled at the older man.

"Mm, that feels nice," said Don, now grinning at Fred.

"Yes, it does feel nice to be in someone's arms," replied Fred.

Don grinned broadly. "I didn't mean that Fred, I was talking about that hardness pressed up against me. That feels good!"

Fred blushed and tried to break free but Don's muscular arms pinned him to the burly man's body.

"I know how frustrated you must feel, Fred, so don't fight it."

Don's mouth moved closer to Fred's. Fred closed his eyes, not out of fear, but more in anticipation. He felt Don's lips touch his and instantly there was a connection between the two men. Their mouths parted and their tongues began searching each other's mouths. With this, their passion increased and their bodies were writhing like wild animals, pressed up against each other. Don's hand went in search and soon found Fred's erection that was pressing up against Don's. He squeezed it and Fred groaned loudly, pressing harder against Don. Don's hand then moved into Fred's shorts and he felt the warmth of Fred's hard penis, which he began stroking slowly. Their mouths continued to fight and Fred's right hand went in search of Don's erection, finding it, and he began stroking it.

Don, in one swift movement, pulled down Fred's shorts, allowing his throbbing penis freedom. Instantly, Don dropped to his knees, placed his mouth around Fred's erect, penis, and started sucking on it. Fred moaned with pleasure and started a slow rhythmic thrust into Don's mouth. Both men were now moaning together and Fred had placed his hands behind Don's head and was pulling his head back and forth, as he sucked.

"Oh yes!" groaned Fred loudly as Don increased his speed.

It did not take Fred long to reach his climax as he was so aroused. He shouted to Don.

"I'm going to come, Don!"

Don continued without taking a break and very soon, Fred was gasping and thrusting all at the same time as he flooded Don's mouth with his seed. Don continued to please Fred without losing contact and when he felt that there was no more seed flowing, he pulled his mouth away and allowed Fred's heavy penis to flop free. Don then stood up, placed a kiss on Fred's lips, pulled him closer to him and then said, "I know how much you needed that, Fred."

Fred was breathing heavily and trying to take the whole experience in at the same time.

"But what about you, Don?"

Don smiled back at Fred.

"This was for you. I know you saw Paul and me in the bedroom and I was sure that it turned you on and I also know that you don't have someone in your life that you can make love to, so this was a little something for you, besides I have Paul to empty my seed into."

Fred felt a little embarrassed by all this, but he had been aroused by seeing Paul and Don together and he had not had any form of sex for a long time, so in a funny way, he felt relieved and happy at the same time.

The two men hugged once more and Fred really did not know what to say to Don, other than "thanks buddy!"

They then left the apartment, locking the front door behind them, went down to Don's truck and drove back to Fred's home.

Would you like to come in Don?" enquired Fred.

"Thanks Fred, but I don't think I will. I should get back to see how Paul is getting on."

"Speaking of Paul," continued Fred, "are you going to tell him what happened today? I just need to know where both he and I stand. I mean, I wouldn't want to say something about today and he became angry."

Don gave a gentle chuckle.

"You have nothing to fear, Fred. Paul is very understanding."

"But what concerns me is that are you going to tell him? After all I have to face him when we're working together and I now know your relationship with Paul."

"As I said, Fred, you have nothing to concern yourself about, and in any case I don't think you really know about my relationship with Paul."

"Oh, I'm sorry if that came across in the wrong way," said Fred apologetically.

"Maybe one day you'll understand our relationship together," answered Don. "Any rate, let me get going and check if he's any better or not. Thanks again Fred and listen, buddy, take good care of yourself."

Fred smiled at Don and winked. Then the muscular builder climbed back into his truck, started it up, revved the engine and, in a cloud of exhaust fumes, sped off.

Fred closed the front door, wandered into the kitchen to get himself a drink and then sat down in the lounge, thinking of what had taken place today.

CHAPTER 7

Fred had gone to bed feeling elated with what had happened between him and Don, albeit brief and unexpected. It was something that Don had said that also jogged his memory and that was that he had no one to love in his life. For a short period, he had been able to share the love that he did have with Patrick, Peter's former sports coach, but after Patrick had departed to go to another college, Fred's love life had died down and he had felt alone again. This was also, why he had suggested to Peter that he get himself a part-time job in order to get out and meet people. Already he had met Don and Paul and he liked both of them for different reasons: Don for his manliness, and Paul for the gentleness that he possessed. They seemed the complete antithesis of each other. Unfortunately, Paul was a bit of a closed book and did not allow himself to be as open as Don. Fred really knew nothing about Paul, other than he appeared to look like a surfer and he had now established that Paul and Don had some sort of relationship, quite what that was like, Fred did not really know. He had merely heard Don mention that they were good friends but that Fred would not understand his relationship with Paul. Fred wondered if they were there to help each other out sexually or maybe they were very close friends but not lovers. On the other hand, he considered whether they were brothers – no, that could never, he thought – they do not look alike and it would be highly unlikely that they were brothers, he convinced himself.

Fred's mind then turned to Don's interpretation of the dream he'd had and wondered if in fact, Don did know anything about dream interpretation or whether he was conning Fred. Don did not seem the type, so he brushed that idea aside. Maybe he was about to meet someone special or his entire love life was about to sink into the oblivion. Oh well, if that was about to happen, he could not complain as he had enjoyed a full life and had enjoyed the sex as well – when it occurred.

His mind flew back to the time he was married to his ex-wife and how they had enjoyed each other and bringing up Peter, how they had attended Peter's swimming galas and how he tried to encourage his only son to do the best he could in every task that he attempted. It was only as Peter got older that he and Fred were drawn closer to each other, and more so once the divorce came through. Then he thought of the times, while still married to his ex-wife, he used to visit his old fire fighter friend so they could pleasure each other by having sex together. A smile broke on his face as his thoughts went back in time. He thought of how he would go out at night, under the guise of some work excuse, and make the visit to his male friend, stay a few hours enjoying happiness and sex, and then return home as though nothing untoward had taken place. It was this that made amends for his frustrations during his married life, he thought, but now he was alone.

He then thought of Patrick. He knew how they had enjoyed each other's love and company. It was strange to Fred, how quickly they had connected and fallen in love; it only took one weekend for them to realise that they had certain things in common and one of those was to love someone unconditionally. They were both divorced, Fred as a result of his pursuit of men and Patrick as his ex wife felt that he spent too much time with his students and not enough time with her. Patrick was the coach to Peter, as well as the college physiotherapist, and therefore knew of Fred before meeting him and Fred, through Peter knew quite a bit about Patrick.

– – – – –

Fred waited for Don and Paul to pick him up for work. Their task was to complete Brad's apartment that they had been working on so that Brad could either move into it, if he so wished, or put it on the market and sell it, fully furnished.

The recognizable "toot" of the truck's horn was heard along with the rattling sound as it drew to a halt outside of Fred's house. Fred closed the front door, locking it and climbed into the front of the truck alongside of Paul and Don.

"Hi Paul, how are you feeling?" enquired Fred, squeezing in the front of the truck.

"Much better, thanks, Fred. I think I just needed a day in bed with medication and I would feel fine."

"Well, I'm glad to see you again up and about, and you're not looking too bad either," added Fred.

"I believe that you helped Don, and you guys managed to finish the kitchen."

"Yes, although I must say, that I did nothing. It was Don who did all the work," replied Fred, not sure if Don had mentioned to Paul what had taken place that day.

"How are you feeling, Fred?" asked Don. "Have you solved your dream yet?"

"No, but I did it some thought."

"Yeah, Don did tell me about your dream and I came up with the same ideas that he had mentioned to you – not that I'm an expert," chuckled Paul, smiling broadly at Fred.

"Well, I cannot think of any other interpretation that could fit the objects that I saw," said Fred, "so I'm more than willing to believe you guys."

Throughout the journey to the apartment, no mention was made of Don and Fred's moment of passion having taken place, and this did not make Fred feel easy. He really wanted to know if Paul was aware of what had happened. It was eating him up, and he was tempted to open his mouth and just tell Paul. He thought that he owed it to the young man, especially if Paul and Don were in a serious relationship together. Don, in the meantime, concentrated on the road ahead of him, not saying a word.

"Paul…," hesitated Fred. "I was thinking…"

"Yes, Fred?"

"Um…"

"I think Fred is hoping that you'll check his work for him," interrupted Don.

"Of course I will, if that's what you want, but I'm sure you did a sterling job."

Fred glanced across to catch Don's eye. Don winked and gave a slight smile, letting Fred know that he would cover for him if anything untoward were said. Fred immediately thought that Don had not said anything to Paul. For the remainder of the journey nothing more was said.

When they arrived at the apartment, they virtually fell from the cramped front of the truck. Don, being the leader and the person with the front door keys, led the way with Paul immediately behind him and Fred following. They opened the apartment front door, went in and closed it behind them.

As they entered the kitchen, Paul gasped and said, "Wow! This looks great, guys. You both did a magnificent job. I love those light fittings, Don. Did you pick them Fred?"

"No, they were here in the second bedroom," said Fred, wondering why Paul had not seen them there when he and Don were "busy" in that room, or was Paul being facetious?

"The only thing we still have to do is sort out the second bedroom and then check that everything is where it should be," said Don, leaving the kitchen and going into the lounge area.

Fred reached what might be considered a "Hamlet" moment,

where he was considering what to do; to tell Paul, what had happened or not. It was a case of to tell or not to tell, that is the question; whether it is nobler in the mind to suffer the rage and anger of Paul, or to keep quiet and remain friends with both men.

Fred was rather hesitant, but he chose to take Don's advice and to keep quiet. He didn't want the two men to become argumentative between themselves, let alone with him.

"Hey you guys!" shouted Don, "Let's get this work done with, then we can get out of here."

Paul and Fred headed on the direction of Don's voice. When they entered the second bedroom, they saw that Don had already positioned the furniture where he thought it should all be placed.

"I think you've done my work for me," said Fred, rather surprised that the furniture in the room looked so well-positioned.

"Well, I wasn't going to wait for you two "ladies" to get your act together."

Don's mention of calling Paul and Fred "ladies" suddenly broke the atmosphere that might have lurked with Fred.

"And who are you calling "ladies"? questioned Fred, with an indignant tone to his voice.

Paul laughed, as he knew that Don was making a joke but was not sure if Fred had taken this name calling seriously.

"I'll show you who are the ladies here, Don," challenged Fred.

"Mm, sounds like Daddy is getting threatening," quipped Don, with a smirk on his face.

Fred could see that Don was teasing him and wondered if it was because of their interaction together.

"You might be all muscle, but I can still hold my own against you, Don," replied Fred with a broad grin, as if taunting the bigger man.

"Hey! Cut it out you guys," intervened Paul, not wanting there to be any fighting taking place.

"It's quite all right, Paul, Fred and I are just joking with each other," confirmed Don.

The "tension" was broken and Fred could see the relief on Paul's face.

At that moment, Fred's mobile phone rang shrilly "Hello, Fred speaking."

"Hi Dad, it's Peter. I'm sorry to trouble you but I've just had a thought about your party. What do you think of having a fancy dress party but based on a fantasy person or thing?"

There was a stunned silence from Fred.

"Are you there, Dad?"

"Yes... I just wasn't sure if I heard you properly. You did say fancy dress based on a fantasy?"

"Yes," replied Peter, excitedly.

"I'm not sure Peter. Just hang on a minute."

Fred held the phone away from his mouth and turned to Don and Paul.

"Listen guys, Peter has this idea for my party – he's thinking of having fancy dress based on a fantasy person or thing. What do you guys think of that?"

Don and Paul looked at each other for a moment, and then like a chorus from some musical show, they both concurred with Peter.

"Are you serious?" questioned Fred to his work mates.

"Yes, absolutely. We think it would be great fun," replied Don.

"Hello Peter. My work buddies seem to think that your idea might be good, although I don't."

"Good! That means that you're outnumbered Dad so it's going to be a fancy dress party and you must come dressed as your fantasy person or thing, sort of like your alter ego, so you had better tell those that you have invited," said Peter finally switching off his phone.

Fred stood there slightly dumbstruck for a moment, and then a broad smile began to appear across his face.

"What's the grin for?" enquired Don.

"I was just thinking about what Peter has just said, and although I was initially a little taken aback by his suggestion, now I think it could be fun."

"I've already decided what I'm, wearing or going as," said Don enthusiastically.

"What?" questioned Paul.

"I think you'd know, but you'll see," replied Don, slapping Paul on the back as he said it.

"What about you, Fred?" enquired Paul.

"I have thought of something, but I'll decide nearer the time."

"In the mean time, I think we should start clearing up here before Brad arrives," said Don.

"Is Brad coming here?" asked Fred.

"Mm, he said he would come round to check up on the apartment," replied Don.

The three men went around the apartment, checking that there were no cables showing, no pieces of furniture unaccounted for and no tools lying around.

They had spent about ten minutes checking everything when they heard Brad's voice from inside of the apartment.

"Where's everyone?" called Brad.

"We're out on the balcony," shouted Don.

Brad made his way to the balcony, observing the layout of the lounge and the positioning of the furniture as he passed through.

"Hi guys. This looks great, from what I've seen so far," said Brad enthusiastically.

"Can we show you around, Brad?" asked Don.

"Sure, lead on."

Don led the way and the others followed him as they went from room to room with Brad "oohing" and "aahing" at what he saw. He seemed impressed by what they had done and this made Fred feel satisfied. At the end of the tour around the apartment, Brad took Fred aside.

"How's it been, Fred?"

"Fine thanks, Brad. I've actually enjoyed myself and I hope I've satisfied you by what I've done here."

"I think you've done a remarkable job. I know that all the furnishings had already been selected so you had nothing like that to do, but on the next project, I'll let you decide on the furnishings and decor."

"Thanks Brad. Oh by the way Peter phoned and he has a plan for my birthday party – he wants to have fancy dress."

"Fancy dress," laughed Brad.

"Yes, but based on a fantasy of your own. In other words come dressed as a person or thing that you fantasize over."

"That sounds like it could be quite kinky," retorted Brad, with a naughty grin on his face. "I'll have to think about that one."

"The one thing that has crossed my mind about this fancy dress party and dressing in your fantasy, is that it might suggest some hidden desire we probably have within us," said Fred, rather contemplatively.

"Meaning what, Fred?" asked Brad.

"Well, think about it. You are probably going to come as someone or something that is repressed within your sub-conscious. Let's say, just for argument's sake, that you come dressed as a… shall we say… a priest."

Brad roared with laughter.

"Not likely," chuckled Brad, trying to control his laughter when he saw the serious look on Fred's face.

"I'm being serious, Brad," retorted Fred. "If you came as a priest, I might think that you had some suppressed desire to either turn your life around so as to become a better person or you might even have a desire to be forgiven for some act that you have committed."

"You mean, like all the boys I've had sex with?" asked Brad, now laughing heartily.

"Maybe not as simple as that," responded Fred, "but I think that maybe there is some hidden aspect within us and it's our way of exposing it to the world without admitting it to anyone."

"Doesn't make sense to me," replied Brad, shaking his head.

"Well, have you thought of how you're coming dressed?" asked Fred.

"Yes, I think so, but I'm not telling you. I want it to be a surprise."

"Fine. Just remind me to explain my theory when I see you at the party," concluded Fred.

"And what are you coming as?" enquired Brad.

Fred smiled back at his friend, shook his head and said, "You'll see at the party!"

"Guys!" shouted Brad, "I'm heading back to the office. Thanks again for the work and I'll be in touch when the next project is ready."

With that, Brad swept out of the apartment, leaving the remaining three men loitering around wondering what to do for the rest of the day.

"I think I'd like to go home, guys. I'd prefer to relax there and maybe have a swim, rather than sitting here doing nothing. If either of you want to come for a swim, you're most welcome," added Fred.

"Sounds like a good idea in this heat. Thanks for the invite, Fred?"

"Not at all, and if you don't have bathing suits, I have extras or you can swim in the nude if you want to."

"Come on Paul. Let's go for a swim at Fred's place."

The three men boarded the truck and chugged their way back to Fred's house for a swim to cool down. When they arrived at the house, Fred offered Don and Paul Speedos, of which he had a number, but both men politely refused.

"No thanks, Fred, if that's okay with you, we're both used to being nude so swimming like that is not an issue with us," replied Don, shucking his jeans to the ground and stepping out of them.

Don then pulled off his shirt and Fred stood admiring the muscular torso that stood before him. Don had a buffed and well defined chest; his biceps bulged and his legs appeared to resemble tree trunks. Fred noticed the two full nipples that had thick metal bars pierced through them and then his eyes fell on the massive bulge that formed in his briefs. Paul, on the other hand, had a more athletic build, resembling what one would expect from a swimmer. Paul had no piercings that Fred could observe, but he looked lean and muscular too. Both men stood there in their briefs while Fred also stripped. At one stage, there was a moment when all three men stood admiring each other's body. Finally, Don was the first to strip completely, and pulled down his briefs and stepped out of them. Fred could not take his eyes from the appendage that hung there – long, cut and thick with another shining metal bar through the head of Don's penis. Don flicked his balls and then added, "Are you two getting undressed or not?"

Paul was next to strip off his briefs, and Fred noticed that he too, was well endowed, except that Paul was uncut. Fred could feel a tingle in his groin by what he was looking at; two handsome men, both well endowed and both naked in front of him. Paul and Don stood waiting for Fred to strip, not only as they wanted to get into the cool water but to see Fred naked.

Fred obliged and Don was the first to pass a comment.

"Very nice body for an old man, hey!"

Paul smiled in approval and said, "Very hot body, Fred. You've obviously looked after yourself."

"Have you been going to the gym?" asked Don, squeezing Fred's biceps.

"No, but way back I did go occasionally," replied Fred.

"Mm! Very nice," continued Don, looking over Fred's naked body. "What do you think, Paul?"

Paul grinned sheepishly as he admired Fred's nakedness.

"I like it very much," replied Paul.

Fred could see that Paul was having a reaction to Fred's nakedness. Paul's penis was slowly beginning to take on a life of its own and he was becoming self-conscious of it. He placed his hands over his ever-burgeoning erection until Don noticed it.

"Put it away, boy! I think you need some of the cold swimming pool water, Paul!"

Paul ran off and dived into the swimming pool, still hiding his erection.

"Tell me, Don," asked Fred as he and Don walked through the house to the pool. "Did that piercing in your cock hurt?"

Don roared with laughter.

"Fred, no pain, no gain! Sure, it hurts a little, but it is what I wanted so I was prepared to endure any pain. It was the same with the nipples, but I think I mentioned earlier that I actually want to get some thicker bars for my nipples."

"But tell me, doesn't the one in your cock affect your feelings there?" asked Fred.

"On the contrary, I have a far greater feeling there. It makes me more horny with that bar through my cockhead." replied Don, lifting his heavy penis to show Fred the metal bar.

The two men reached the swimming pool and dived in to join Paul.

"So tell me, boy, have you lost that hard-on, eh?"

Paul blushed as both Fred and Don laughed at his predicament.

"You see what happens to him when he sees a hot naked man, Fred?"

"I wouldn't say hot," retorted Fred.

"Rubbish! You would give any younger guy a good run for his money when it comes to sex appeal," said Don, winking at Fred.

Fred was wondering if Don was making a move on him again, except this time in front of Paul. Whatever the motive, Fred was not about to have a threesome in the pool or in the house with his two work buddies. He liked both men, but felt that he didn't know them well enough, even though Don had sucked him off and that in itself might be construed as "knowing" someone well enough.

"I don't know so much about that, but if you say so, then I'll believe you," laughed Fred.

"Don't you think Fred's got sex appeal, Paul?"

Paul blushed at being asked such a direct question.

"Sure," answered Paul, smiling at Fred. "I'm positive any guy, young or old would go for him."

"There you go, Fred. Even Paul thinks you have sex appeal, so you've had a young and an older guy's opinions."

"Well thanks, guys, I appreciate your views, but for whatever reason, I'm not on the market," said Fred with a glint in his eyes.

He really had not thought about looking for someone after Patrick had left and although there were times when he felt lonely, he got over the loneliness and survived another day. Don had sidled up closer to Fred and whispered to him, "Want some fun with us?"

Don's question left Fred a little taken aback. Fred then looked towards Paul who was leaning against the side of the swimming pool, gazing at Fred as though in a trance. Fred felt Don's hand brush against his stomach and the sudden touch gave him a fright, which caused him to gasp. Paul's trance was broken. He smiled towards Fred. Don never let up and let his hand drift under the water until he could feel Fred's slowly hardening penis. Don gave it a squeeze in his hand and again Fred gasped. The feeling was sending erotic waves through his body, but he was unsure how to deal with the situation.

Don leaned in closely to Fred's face and whispered, "Do you want me to fuck you?"

Fred was by now becoming a little frantic. Yes, he enjoyed the attention he was getting from Don, but he felt it was wrong to be doing all this in front of Paul, who remained against the side of the pool, smiling.

"I don't think so, Don, but thanks for the offer," replied Fred, swallowing hard as he felt his penis getting harder with the anticipation of what could happen.

Don was not about to give up his pursuit.

"Do you want to fuck Paul?" he asked Fred.

"No thanks, Don. I think I should actually be getting out and dry myself," replied Fred, hoisting himself out of the pool, near to where Paul was situated. As Fred emerged from the water, Paul could see the fully erect penis and knew immediately that Don had been making a move on Fred. He was not angered in any way but was more intrigued by the size of Fred's erect penis. Fred immediately wrapped a towel around his waist to cover his embarrassment and seated himself on a chair alongside of the swimming pool.

Don, in the meantime swam across to where Paul was resting against the side of the pool. He positioned himself in front of Paul and Fred could see how Don pressed his body up against Paul's. He watched, fascinated as Don began to writhe his body against Paul's and he knew what was happening under the surface of the water, but he could not bring himself to look away.

Don locked lips with Paul, and they started to kiss passionately and all the while, their bodies continued to writhe together. Fred had his muscular arms around Paul's neck and was hugging him, but Paul's hands were down his side under the water. Fred wondered if Paul was feeling Don's thick penis under the water, but he could not see. After some time of kissing, their lips parted and with his huge hands and muscular arms, Don turned Paul around so he faced away from the pool. Don repositioned himself up against Paul's back and from the movement of the water, Fred was well aware that Don was trying to sink his hard, thick penis into Paul. Paul gave a loud groan and then the water began to splash and churn from their body movements as Don fucked Paul against the swimming pool wall.

Fred sat, fascinated by their action and started to stroke his own erection still hidden under his towel. Paul and Don worked their way to the shallow end of the swimming pool at this point, Paul knelt on the top step and Fred could clearly see Don's massive penis sliding in and out of the younger man's ass while Paul groaned with each thrust.

Fred was completely transfixed by the scene playing out in front of him. It was as if he had been hypnotized or glued to the spot where he was, as he did not move, other than his hand that was stroking his penis furiously.

As Don fucked Paul, he took hold of Paul's bouncing penis and started stroking it in rhythm with his thrusts. Both men were breathing heavily as they performed for Fred. Both men were nearing their climax and so was Fred.

It was Paul who was the first to climax with a loud cry and that was followed closely by a deep growl and a grunt from Don as he filled Paul's ass with his warm semen. By this time, Fred was also breathing frantically and he dropped his towel to the ground, stood up and, stroking his engorged penis, fired his load onto the paving around the swimming pool. Both Don and Paul smiled as they saw the pleasure across Fred's face; and how his penis continued to ooze semen while Fred slowly began to get his breath back.

Once they had all expended themselves and were more relaxed, Fred spoke for the first time after a long period of silence.

"Would either of you like something to drink?"

"I think we all need something, Fred," responded Don, giving Paul a loving slap on the butt and slowly pulling his penis from Paul's warm ass.

Paul and Don both emerged from the pool, dried themselves and wrapped the towels around their waists. Their still hard penises tented the towels as they followed Fred back into the house. Fred handed a bottle to each of them and then they sat down in the kitchen to enjoy their beers.

"Don, do you mind if I ask a personal question?" asked Fred.

"Sure, no problem,"

"Are you and Paul in a relationship?"

Don smiled at Paul and then answered.

"Not in the sense you're probably thinking. We're fuck buddies, aren't we Paul?"

Paul nodded in agreement.

"How long have you been fuck buddies?" continued Fred.

"I'm not sure, but a pretty long time," added Don.

Fred nodded that he understood, but was still a little unsure of how they interpreted the meaning of "fuck buddies".

"But if you have been together for a long time as you say, don't you have feelings for each other, and if you do then I cannot understand how you can still say that you're fuck buddies. To me a fuck buddy is someone who you have sex with occasionally but with no strings attached and with that, no feelings. How could you be intimate with someone yet retain nothing but feelings of pure lust for them? If you didn't like them, you wouldn't continue with the arrangement no matter how "hot", "hung" or "handsome" they were. In other words, isn't there a risk that you start to develop some sort of feelings for them – at which point they are no longer just a "fuck buddy" and start to become a romance?"

"But if Paul wants to go with someone else, that's fine by me," said Don.

"What I'm trying to understand is how you can call yourselves fuck buddies when there are definitely emotions between you. Don't you feel emotionally for Don, Paul?"

"Of course I do, but we don't live together," replied Paul.

"But Paul, I don't live with anyone but I have emotional feelings for someone and I don't see that person as a fuck buddy."

"Oh!" exclaimed Don. "So there is someone in your life after all?"

"No, no! What I mean is that I love someone but we are not living together."

"But are you having sex with him or her?" questioned Don.

"No we're not."

"Then you don't have a fuck buddy. I think you're getting yourself muddled, Fred," said Don, kindly.

Fred thought about what he had just unwittingly said. He had openly admitted that he loved someone. Although he had not named the person to Don or Paul, he knew in his heart who he meant.

"I think to sum it up, Fred, Paul and I have sex together, but we don't live together like a couple and when we feel like sex we have it and then go our own ways."

Fred smiled, acknowledging that he understood their arrangement, even if he didn't necessarily agree with it, and took another sip of his beer.

After they had finished their beers, Paul and Don dressed again, thanked Fred and departed in a cloud of exhaust fumes as the truck chugged off.

CHAPTER 8

The night of the party arrived, but not before Keith, Peter and Fred had gone to see their show as part of his birthday celebration. Peter had arranged for drinks and food to be delivered to Fred's house and stored there for the party later.

The plan was for Fred to meet the other two at the theatre and then, head back to Fred's house to await the guests. Fred had laid out his outfit for the fancy dress party so he could get changed once he returned home from the theatre, and had placed the drinks that needed chilling, into his fridge. The food had been placed on the dining room table and a dresser in the dining room. Everything appeared to be ready to celebrate his sixty-fifth birthday.

Fred had no idea as to how many people would be attending the party, except that he had noticed an abundant amount of food and drink had been delivered, so he assumed that Peter had invited quite a few of his friends. From Fred's invitations, he knew that Brad, Don and Paul were coming, so he could account for them, plus himself and Keith and Peter.

Peter had told him to dress casually for the theatre performance, which he duly did. Fred climbed into his car and drove the short distance

to the centre of the local village. The address that Peter had given him was
a local bar and apparently, a small theatre had been created in the upstairs
section of the bar.

Fred arrived at the bar to see quite a number of people both
gathered inside, drinking and many more outside smoking and merely
chatting, some with drinks in their hands. Fred found parking, got out of
his car, locked it and ventured into the bar. He looked around to see if he
could see Peter, but to no avail, so he wandered over to the bar counter to
order a drink.

"Can I help you, sir," shouted the barman, a young, long haired
man of about thirty.

"Could I have a beer, please," shouted Fred, over the din of chatter
and laughter coming from within the bar.

The beer duly arrived and the barman received his payment for it.
Fred eased his way through the thronging crowd and found a spot near the
entrance to the bar and stood there surveying the crowd while sipping his
beer.

The crowd of people tended to be about Peter's age or a little older,
but Fred didn't notice any of his age. This was obviously a popular spot
for the younger generation, he thought. As he stood there, he noticed a few
men started eyeing him and talking among themselves, obviously about
him. He wondered if it was because he looked so out of place with the
general age group of those present. He started to become a little self-
conscious but chose not to let it get to him.

After having stood near the door for a while, sipping his beer, a
young man in his early twenties approached Fred.

"Hi, are you alone?" asked the young man.

"Hi. I'm actually waiting for someone," replied Fred.

"Oh, I'm sorry," said the young man apologetically and sounding
a little let down.

"Not a problem," continued Fred. "It seems that the bar is quite
busy tonight. Do you come here often?" enquired Fred.

"No, not really. It is just that I thought I would come and see the play tonight. Are you also going to see it?"

"Yes. In fact it's my son and his boyfriend that I'm waiting for, as they're taking me to the play."

"Oh, so you're married?" asked the young man with a little trepidation mixed with a sense of exhilaration in his voice.

"No, divorced. My wife found out that I liked men and so she dumped me. Well, not really dumped, that's the wrong word."

The young man's face lit up on hearing this information.

Fred noticed the change in the young man's expression and immediately realised that the young man was hoping to have a date with Fred, so that he could boast to his gay friends that he had been out with a "straight" man! Fred smiled to himself as he attempted to visualize the young man's enthusiasm in telling his friends about their meeting.

"Do you have a boyfriend?" asked the young man, sidling a little closer to Fred, and using the excuse of the crowded bar as the reason that he was having to move closer.

"No!" replied Fred, grinning from ear to ear as he humored the young man.

"Oh!" cooed the young man and smiling profusely. He touched Fred on the arm and asked, "Do you have a ticket? If not, I'll get another and you can sit next to me."

Fred politely told the young man that Peter, his son had the tickets, so he had no idea where they would be sitting in the theatre. It was at that point that Fred saw Peter and Keith arrive in the bar and waved to them.

"My son has just arrived," Fred, told the young man, who immediately looked around the bar to see if he could see Peter.

Peter and Keith battled their way through the heaving throng of humanity and eventually arrived where Fred was standing. Peter hugged and kissed his father and Fred shook hands with Keith.

"Hi Dad, sorry that we're a bit late," apologized Peter, "but I see you've already made friends," indicating with a slight nod of his head towards the young man.

"Oh yes! I don't know who he is but I think he's after me," chuckled Fred.

"It's a compliment when a younger guy goes after an older guy, Fred," said Keith, putting an arm around Peter's shoulders.

"I'm glad that you said older and not old, as I don't consider myself as being old, and certainly not after my young neighbor made passes at me," said Fred, smiling to the young man who was still standing nearby.

"You're not old, Fred," continued Keith. "You would actually be quite surprised how many younger guys are chasing after older men, as they see them as being more experiences and more stable. It's the younger ones who flit from one relationship to another," said Keith, offering his wisdom.

"I'm sure that they do," responded Fred. "But it does feel good when someone much younger takes an interest in you. Maybe I'm not used to this and maybe that's also a reason why I wanted to get another job so as to meet more people. I suppose I should get used to people talking to me or even making a pass at me," laughed Fred.

"So, aren't you going to introduce us to him, Dad?"

Fred laughed heartily. "I don't even know his name."

Keith eyed the young man, smiled at him and winked.

"Now, are you making a pass at him?" enquired Fred, who noticed Keith's action.

"No, but he does seem quite cute," replied Keith.

Both Fred and Peter glanced at each other and then at the young man, wondering whether Keith was going to start up a conversation with him or not.

"Do you have the tickets?" asked Fred, trying to change the topic and get away from the young man.

"Yes, but we're expecting another guest, who might be inside already," said Peter, looking around the bar.

Keith seemed reluctant to leave the bar area and the young man, who had sidled up closer to Keith.

Fred found it odd that Keith tended to be hovering in the background and he was not sure as to why. He wondered if Peter had mentioned their conversation about Keith or was it Keith's mission to make contact with the young man and possibly set up a date with him, but Fred was determined not to let anything ruin his night.

"We'll get drinks at the interval," said Peter, "as the play is about to start."

"Where do we go?" asked Fred.

"Upstairs, Dad. Come on, follow me," said Peter, starting to lead the way, with Keith and Fred following, and not very far behind them, the young man.

They entered the upstairs area, which resembled more an acting area, than a theatre. The space consisted of a long rectangular area for the action and adjacent to it were raised tiers of seating, for the audience. There was no proscenium nor curtain breaking the "stage" from the audience so when they entered; they saw the stage setting with all the props already placed for the performance. They carried the remains of their beers with them and Peter led the way to their seats, which were in the central area of the front rows. As they neared their seat, Fred stopped and stared ahead of him. Peter continued to their seats and waited for Fred and Keith to follow.

Fred's stare turned into a slight smile and then the longer he stared, so his smile broadened to a grin and then sheer laughter as he rushed forward.

"Patrick, is that you?" shouted Fred, as he reached Peter and looked at the man sitting next to their vacant seats.

Patrick rose from his seat, smiled back at Fred, flung his arms wide and embraced Fred warmly.

"Yes, Fred, it's me," replied Patrick, hugging Fred tightly to him and eventually their lips met and remained together for a very long time.

"Hey, break it up guys," said Peter, "people will think that you're part of the act."

Finally both Fred and Patrick restrained themselves and sat down.

"What are you doing here, Patrick?" asked Fred excitedly.

"Happy birthday, Honey. I'm your birthday present."

"You're what!" exclaimed the dumbfounded Fred.

"Peter contacted me and told me it was your birthday and asked if I would like to attend. Now, what an invitation is that? Could I refuse? Never! So here I am."

Once more Fred leaned across and hugged Patrick.

"Now you have made my day for me. This is the best birthday present anyone could get," said Fred, obviously fighting back tears of joy. "You don't know how I have missed you, buddy."

"Me too," answered Patrick. "When I left, my life felt so empty. Even though I met new people where I went, it was not the same. You made a great impact on my life, Fred, and I regret leaving."

"Well, I also regretted you leaving. It was so lonely without you, and I think even Peter knew it as I was taking things out on him so unnecessarily, but it's so good to have you here now. I hope that you're coming to the party after the show."

"I wouldn't miss it for the world," replied Patrick.

"But how have you been? You look so handsome still and ... have you been working out?" asked Fred.

"Yes, as I also became lonely without you, so to take my mind off missing you, I enrolled at a gym and spent my spare time there."

"Well, you're really looking good," said Fred, beaming and taking Patrick's hand and holding it in his and feeling the warmth flow from one to the other.

Peter and Keith merely smiled at one another as the two former lovers rekindled their love. However, Keith did venture a glance around the seating area to see who was arriving for the show, and happened to see the young man from the bar. Keith smiled at him and the young man reciprocated with a smile.

The lights to the venue dimmed and the play started.

"I can't even remember what this play is called," whispered Fred to Patrick, still holding his hand.

"It's called "Stark Raving Naked", which is what we should be," said Patrick, squeezing Fred's hand.

"You're so right," responded Fred, giving Patrick's hand a squeeze too.

The lead actor entered the acting area, positioned himself, holding a telephone receiver and started his dialogue. Fred glanced to the other actor who had also entered the scene and turned to Peter.

"Isn't that what's his name... you know, Brad's boyfriend?" asked Fred, whispering so as not to be heard by the actors who were literally two or three feet from the front row.

"Yes, it's Phil," whispered Peter.

"I'm glad to see he's working," continued Fred, "as the last time I saw him, he and Brad were fighting because he couldn't get a job."

Fred found himself battling to concentrate on the dialogue being delivered in the play as he was still so excited at being in Patrick's company. Their hands remained clasped as they sat watching the action and occasionally glancing towards each other and smiling lovingly.

The play was divided into a series of short scenes followed by a quick blackout to suggest a lapse in time, and each time there was a blackout, Fred would steal a quick kiss from Patrick.

Eventually, the interval came.

"Are we going downstairs to get drinks?" asked Peter, rising from his seat and seeing his Dad and Patrick still holding hands. A warm loving feeling filled Peter at seeing his Dad so happy.

"Why don't you guys go downstairs and Patrick and I will stay here to chat," suggested Fred. "Do you want a drink, Patrick?"

"Beer would be fine for me please," replied Patrick.

"Make that two, Peter," added Fred.

"I was also wondering, do you think I should invite Phil if he wants to come to the party, Dad?"

"That's up to you Peter, but I thought that he and Brad were no longer together?"

"I just thought it might be a nice idea, and who knows, maybe he and Brad could get back together," laughed Peter as he headed off to get the drinks.

Peter and Keith ventured downstairs while Patrick and Fred remained totally in their own world.

"You don't know how good it is to see you again," said Fred, placing an arm around Patrick's shoulder and drawing him closer towards him.

"I really have missed you, Fred. Life wasn't the same without you, and I must tell you something else..."

Fred tensed a little as he was not sure what news Patrick was about to share with him.

"I have resigned my job, Fred."

"Why?"

"If I told you, I don't think you'd believe me."

"Try me."

"I wanted to move back to you, but never had the courage."

"Why not?"

"I wasn't sure if you'd want me back, not that I did anything to make you think like that, but it did enter my head. Added to that, I wasn't sure if you might have met someone new and they were now part of your life."

"Rubbish! Of course I would have taken you back with open arms," said Fred, pulling Patrick closer to him in a protective manner.

"Well, it wasn't that we parted as enemies, in fact it was quite the opposite, but I thought that maybe you had moved on and found someone else with whom to share your life."

"Patrick, you know how much joy you brought into my life. Even Peter was aware of it. If I am perfectly honest with you, I do not think I would want to spend my life with anyone else. We have so much in common and we have experienced so much together, that I think we know what we like and what we do not like. It's not like starting a relationship for the first time."

"When I hear you talk like that, it sounds to me as if you would like me back in your life!"

Fred looked deeply into Patrick's eyes. "Would you consider coming back to me and us carrying on from where we left off?"

"Are you really being serious?"

"Absolutely, provided you think you can still live with me," said Fred. "Oh, and one other thing, do you think you could live with me holding down a job, albeit a part-time job?"

Patrick laughed loudly and moved closer to Fred to give him a kiss. They wrapped their arms around each other and kissed, oblivious of those left upstairs watching them.

Meanwhile downstairs, Peter had gone off to find the manager in order to get a message to Phil, asking if he wanted to go to the party after the show, and while he did that, Keith had pushed his way through the crowd to the bar counter to order the drinks.

"I hope that you're buying one for me?" said a voice behind Keith.

He turned to see who was speaking. Then he noticed the smiling face of the young man who had been speaking to Fred earlier.

"What are you drinking?" asked Keith.

"G and T please," replied the young man, beaming at Keith. "Where are your friends?"

"They're upstairs and my partner's looking for the manager," answered Keith. "Are you here by yourself?"

"Yes. Always by myself," said the young man, almost oozing self-pity.

Keith received the drinks from the barman and handed the gin and tonic to the young man, who thanked him with a kiss on the cheek.

"You're welcome," said Keith, holding the beers in one hand and glasses in the other. "What's your name?"

"Simon," replied the young man.

"And what do you do, Simon?"

"I'm a student at the local university."

"Oh, that sounds interesting. What are you studying?"

"English and History of Art," said Simon, proudly. "I'm in my final year."

"That's good. Then what are you going to do once you graduate?"

Simon giggled. "I haven't given it a thought."

"So does that mean that you have quite a bit of free time during the day?" asked Keith.

"Some days, yes. Friday's I don't have any lectures so I usually sleep in late, then maybe go to movies."

"That sounds like a lovely life," joked Keith. "Maybe we should meet up some time."

"That would be nice," replied Simon, "but what about your partner?"

"Oh he's at work every day."

"Don't you work?" asked Simon.

"Yes. I do photography, and I was wondering if you'd like to model for me?"

Simon's face lit up. "What sort of photography do you do?"

"Nudes, landscapes, anything in fact," replied Keith.

"Nudes!" exclaimed Simon. "And doesn't your partner mind?"

"He doesn't really worry as he knows I do it professionally. Would you like to model for me as you look as if you have a very nice body?"

"I think that sounds awesome," replied Simon. "Will you let me know when?"

"Well as you said you don't have lectures on a Friday, how about next Friday morning, say 10am?"

"That would suit me, thanks. Must I bring anything?"

"Maybe a change of clothes, so we can take a variety of shots, not all in the same clothes."

"I thought you said you did nudes?"

"Yes, but I think we should also do some clothed shots as well."

At that moment, Peter returned to help carry the drinks upstairs. On seeing the young Simon standing talking to Keith, Peter greeted him.

"Are you enjoying the show?" questioned Peter.

"Oh yes, very much," replied Simon. "Well, I suppose I should be heading back to my seat. I'll see you next week."

At that, Simon left the two men standing in the bar.

"What did he mean by that, Keith?"

"He's agreed to model for me, so I'm taking some shots of him next Friday," replied Keith, without elaborating.

"Oh! I suppose that's fine then," was all Peter was able to say.

They headed back upstairs to give Fred and Patrick their drinks.

"I thought you guys were brewing the hops to make the beer," said Fred jokingly.

"No, it was busy downstairs," said Peter handing round the drinks.

Once Keith and Peter were seated, Fred turned to Peter and whispered in his ear, "Patrick has resigned his job and he wants to come back to me."

Peter saw the smile, not only on Fred's face but in his eyes as well and was about to say something to Patrick, when Fred placed a finger on Peter's lips as if to motion that he keep quiet about it.

"Did you manage to speak to Phil?"

"No, but I gave the manager a message to pass on to him, so we'll have to wait until the end of the show."

"What do you think of it so far?" asked Patrick.

"Well, I wasn't expecting full frontal nudity, but I must say that the guy playing the part of Nick sure has a fine body," remarked Fred.

"Now there's a job for you, Dad, being a part-time masseur," quipped Peter.

"You're right, son, maybe I should consider that," retorted Fred, playing along with Peter's comment.

"I'm not joking, Dad. I think you would do a roaring business. You've got the looks, the body and you'd make money too."

"What do you think, Patrick?" asked Fred.

"I don't think I'd like it if we were in a relationship like the two characters in the play are, but I suppose if you were on your own, it could be a source of income..."

"... and men!" responded Peter, very quickly.

"You see Peter, it wouldn't work for me. Patrick doesn't approve."

Both Patrick and Peter glanced at Fred, rather surprisingly at Fred's comment that Patrick would not approve should they be in a relationship. Was Fred thinking along those lines of restarting the relationship that he had enjoyed with Patrick prior to the younger man's departure to another college?

"What do you think of Phil's acting, Dad?"

"I must say, I am very surprised. I remember how, when we had that weekend at my old house, that Brad, not the character, had run him down and mocked him about his "inability to get a job" and "how he wasn't very good at what he did". I think that was the way that Brad described him. I didn't think that was what Phil was like, so he must have modeled his part on Brad, don't you think?"

"I'm sure that he must have," replied Peter. "Oh, by the way, Dad, in this act we meet an old friend of the two main characters, Michael and Brad."

"Your point being?"

"I'm sure that the playwright wrote the character with you in mind," said Peter, with a grin from ear to ear.

"And how would you know?"

"I know the guy who wrote the play and he told me what it was all about and gave me some insight into the characters."

"So did he say "I wrote this part with your Dad in mind"?"

"Of course not, but the way he described the character, I just think it fits you."

"Well we'll see when he comes on stage."

The lights dimmed once more and the audience settled down for the second half of the play.

When the character that Peter had referred to as being like his father entered the stage, Fred gave a slight guffaw and turned to Peter.

"Are you serious?" whispered Fred to Peter. "He's so flamboyant and camp and I'm sure I'm not like that."

"Not in appearance, but apparently in character," whispered Peter.

Fred sat listening to the dialogue that the old man, Barry, was speaking, to hear if what he said might compare with the way Fred spoke and the things that he said were similar.

The dialogue of Barry, the character, seemed to be very sardonic and Fred wondered if in fact, he was like that.

"Do you think I'm really like that?" whispered Fred to Peter.

Peter merely smiled and nodded.

As the dialogue between the characters Michael and Barry continued, the audience were in fits of laughter and it was at this point that Peter turned to Fred and said, "You see, he is like you, funny and always has an answer to everything."

The dialogue between these two characters continued rapidly:

BARRY: *Oh, and don't forget the "tight little ass"... Darling Brad does have a sexy tight little ass, doesn't he?*

MICHAEL: *Yes... I mean no; this is serious Barry...*

BARRY: *Dear boy, please just humor me. It's not often that I get to hear such romantic language spoken these days.*

MICHAEL: *But Barry this is serious.*

BARRY: *I quite agree, dear boy. Seeing a tight ass these days is serious.*

MICHAEL: *If Brad is seeing other guys behind my back then he's nothing more than a slut.*

BARRY: Don't be too cruel on the young boy, Michael. You know slut is such a harsh word. In my time, no one would have used that word.

MICHAEL: But you once told me you slept with hundreds of men.

BARRY: So I did, but darling, that did not make me a slut. They were friends! When one has sex with a friend, one is not being a slut, one is merely communicating with a close friend, and after all, one needs to stay in touch with friends.

As the actors spoke these lines, a loud roar of laughter reverberated around the venue.

The audience had warmed to the play, but as it progressed, there were lines spoken that could very well have impacted on various members of the audience, depending on the veracity of the lines in relation to their own personal lives. Fred's mind wandered for a moment to Keith and wondered if some of what was being said was having an impact on him or not.

BARRY: Be gentle with the dear boy. After all, you do love him and he is very sweet.

MICHAEL: At the moment I could strangle him, especially if he has been seeing the person behind my back. ... Oh my God!

BARRY: What?

MICHAEL: I have suddenly realised whose voice that was on the answering machine.

BARRY: Whose?

MICHAEL: I had a new client yesterday. An Italian guy...

BARRY: Ooh and Italians are built like studs ...

MICHAEL: *... he's very hunky and I let Brad give him a massage...*

BARRY: *So?*

MICHAEL: *I happened to walk in and Brad was ... well, busy giving him a blowjob... and I interrupted them.*

BARRY: *Oh how delicious. Did you join in?*

MICHAEL: *Barry, this is serious.*

Fred thought of Peter and Keith, not that he was aware that such a situation had arisen between them, but he did have his suspicions. Fred glanced across to where Peter and Keith were sitting to see if there had been any reaction, but neither man looked at each other, so Fred thought that perhaps such a thing may not have happened and that he was just imagining things.

The play continued, filled with laughter and moments of quiet reflection as the dialogue continued until the end when the character Michael faced the audience and spoke directly to them:

MICHAEL: *What would you have done...? It's easy to lay all the blame at his door, but perhaps I had something to do with it as well... I love him you know... Have I got the wrong attitude and am I too stifling in my ways?... Am I taking my job too seriously and should I loosen up like Barry says? ... Being in a relationship is not easy. There have to be boundaries or rules, but how strict must those rules be?... The nature of my job is such that I could have any guy who wants it... They lie on my table, baring their souls and bodies to me. They are entirely in my hands, and my hands can go anywhere the client wants them to go, but I have chosen to withhold... Am I wrong to do that?... What harm will it do if my hands slip somewhere that the client gets pleasure?... Is that not what massaging is about, bringing pleasure to someone?... Will it give me pleasure?... What do you think? ... Maybe Barry and Brad are right. Maybe I need to lighten up a bit...*

*I suppose it wasn't that hard for me to lighten up to Nick
tonight, but then I think the circumstances allowed for that...
Or am I making convenient excuses for that?... Nick's actually
a very nice person... I think I'd like to see him more often...
Who knows – maybe Brad can have his Paulo and I can have
my Nick... Do you think that will work?... I'll sleep on it and
see in the morning... In the meantime, you also sleep on it and
think about it in the morning. Goodnight. Sleep well.*

The lights on the stage area blacked out and the audience broke into thunderous applause as the actors quickly assembled on stage in the darkness to take their bows to the audience. As the lights came back on, the row of actors stood there smiling at their audience, then together they bowed in acknowledgement. Phil caught sight of Fred and Peter in the front row and beamed at them, winking as he did so. The audience was now standing applauding as each actor stepped forward to take an individual bow. When the actor playing the old man Barry stepped forward, there were loud cheers from the gays in the audience as they identified with him and loved his repartee. Naturally, both of the leads got roars of approval and one could see the joy on Phil's face at the recognition he was receiving.

There was another blackout and when the venue light came back on, the cast had disappeared and the audience were very talkative as they slowly made their way back downstairs to the bar area for drinks and the hope of meeting the cast.

Fred led their party downstairs and on the way down asked Peter if they wanted to stay and have a drink.

"I don't think so, Dad, as we must get back to the house for your party. If you'd like, you and Patrick go on ahead and Keith and I will wait for Phil and see if he wants to come to the party."

"I just need to get my bag from your car, Peter," said Patrick.

"Bag?" said Fred, a little surprised.

"Yes, your son invited me to your birthday party and I was told it was fancy dress based on a fantasy, so my bag contains my costume," answered Patrick, with a slight smirk of delight on his face.

Fred and Patrick collected the bag from Peter's car and then made their way to Fred's car, climbed in and got on their way back to Fred's house.

"What did you think of the play, Fred?"

"I actually enjoyed it. I had a great laugh and it was very thought provoking. What about you?"

"I loved it. I particularly liked the old man."

"Yes, but you've always liked older men, haven't you?" laughed Fred, placing a hand on Patrick's leg as he drove.

"Only some older men," replied Patrick, slipping his hand between Fred's thighs.

"Careful where you put your hand," said Fred, jokingly. "You never know what might happen!"

Meanwhile, back in the bar, Peter was waiting near the door that led to where the actors had their dressing rooMs. Keith had once more been in conversation with young Simon who had spotted him and made a hurried move to get near Keith. Peter noted that they were in deep conversation and wondered what plans were being made. He also remembered some of the dialogue from the play and began to wonder how much of the play was taking place in front of him right now. He did not have long to wait, when Phil appeared through the doorway. Peter and Phil hugged each other and Peter congratulated Phil on an excellent performance.

"I hope you enjoyed it, Peter? I know it's a very different type of play, but it sure was fun being in it and the rest of the cast have been so wonderful," said Phil, enthusing about the production.

"So tell me Phil, when you're on stage and the guys playing the ones being massaged, don't they get a hard-on?" asked Peter.

Phil laughed. "You should have seen them in rehearsal. There were times when we had to stop as we were laughing so much and there were times when we would be naughty with the guys, nibbling their cocks, particularly in the blackouts."

"That sounds like great fun," said Keith, ignoring his new friend

Simon to listen more to Phil's story. "I must say that some of those guys in the play are really hot."

"Mm, they are, but they're not all available," continued Phil.

"Meaning what?" enquired Peter.

"Well, the guys that played Michael, my partner and the older guy who played Barry, are both married."

"Are you serious about the Michael character?" asked Keith, somewhat surprised. "I thought he was gay and the older guy, well I'm not into older guys, but he played his part so well, I could have sworn he was a natural born gay."

"No," laughed Phil. "As I say both are married, but I don't think that excludes them completely as the chap playing Michael is always teasing and flirting with me, so who knows."

"Maybe you'll get lucky with him," said Keith.

"Tell me, Phil, did you get my message I sent during the interval?"

"Yes I did, thanks Peter, but tell me, who is going to be there?" enquired Phil.

"Obviously we'll be there and my Dad and Patrick, and I believe my Dad invited Brad along."

There was a stunned silence as the last words spoken penetrated Phil's mind. Very quickly, he responded.

"Thanks Peter, but I don't think I'll take up the offer."

"Because of Brad?" questioned Peter.

Phil merely nodded his head. "Please wish your Dad Happy Birthday from me, but I think I'll just head home."

Peter said that he understood how Phil would feel seeing Brad and them being in such close confines in the house, but he said he would pass on Phil's message to his Dad. They said their goodbyes, after which Keith excused himself for a moment, under the guise that he needed to go to the toilet and returned a while later with young Simon in tow. Peter looked more than surprised to see him and wondered what Keith had said to the young man.

"Keith, what is he doing here?" whispered Peter to his partner, so Simon would not hear.

"I thought as Phil was not coming to the party, we could take Simon along."

"But Keith, we don't even know him."

"All the more reason to take him and find out about him."

"But surely not at my Dad's birthday party?"

"I can't see why not?" retorted Keith. "He can come as our guest."

"But I don't even know him."

Keith seemed to ignore Peter's pleas and the three of them climbed into the car and set off to Peter's home to get changed.

CHAPTER 9

Fred and Patrick arrived back at Fred's house and were the only ones there as none of the other guests had yet arrived for the party at that stage. It was 8:30pm when they parked the car and made their way into the house.

"This is new, isn't it Fred?"

"Yes. When you left, I was still in the old house. I felt that after you left, I wanted to be nearer people and not so much on my own. That's how much I missed you," said Fred, embracing Patrick and pulling him closer to him. "I really have missed you, my darling," said Fred, kissing Patrick passionately.

Their mouths locked and their tongues searched each other's mouth and their bodies ground together, Fred thrusting his ever-growing penis against Patrick's hardening penis.

"You know I want you," breathed Fred, as his lips broke free from Patrick's.

"And I want you too, Fred. I have longed for you since the day I left. Those first few nights alone in my bed, were the worst as I cried myself to sleep each night. I longed to feel your strong, warm body pressed tightly against mine, your arms wrapped around my body and to feel you breathing on the back of my neck."

"I feel just as much as you do, Patrick. Not having you share my bed was like some lost soul wandering aimlessly in a desert, not knowing from day to day where I was going. My world felt isolated and empty and even Peter knew how I felt without having to tell him. You being here tonight is the best birthday present I could ever wish for, and knowing that I have you in my arms now fills me to overflowing with joy and happiness," said Fred, kissing Patrick gently on the lips and then the neck. His mouth moved to Patrick's earlobe where Fred nibbled gently and whispered in Patrick's ear, "I love you, my darling."

"And I love you dearly, Fred," whispered Patrick feeling safe and warm in Fred's muscular arMs. "Do you know that I haven't had sex since leaving you."

Fred smiled to himself and cuddled closer to Patrick.

"Do you think we have time to go to the bedroom and make love?" asked Fred.

Patrick chuckled.

"What a question! I would love that, but aren't your guests arriving soon?"

"You're right, but you have got me so horny right now that I wouldn't worry about my birthday or the guests," said Fred, laughing.

"Are we going to spend the night together?" enquired Patrick.

"You are not only going to spend the night, but the rest of your life here with me," said Fred, firmly and determinedly. "I'm not letting you go again. You are staying with me," he continued, kissing and caressing Patrick, running his strong hands over Patrick's chest, firm butt until they reached the bulge that Fred felt pressing up against him. He squeezed Patrick's erect, hard penis and said, "I want this and I want that firm tight ass of yours too."

"You can have both, replied Patrick, breathing heavily as he felt the tingles of pleasure speed through his excited body. "Why did you not write or try to contact me?" asked Patrick.

"I got the feeling that you wanted to break up with me and that's why you took the transfer to the other college," replied Fred.

Patrick hung his head, almost as if in shame.

"I never wanted to leave you, Fred. I felt after my divorce that I needed to have a complete break, to get away from this town, the memories. But not from you. I knew that I could not expect you to move with me and so I realised that the only solution was to leave on my own. Can you forgive me for that?"

"There is nothing to forgive, my darling. I fully understand why you left. It is just that I wished you had spoken to me at the time and explained it all then we could have made a plan," answered Fred, kissing Patrick's forehead gently.

They stood together hugging each other and kissing, but neither spoke again. There was no need to speak as their bodies spoke for them. After what seemed an eternity of kissing and hugging, Fred whispered in Patrick's ear, "I think we need to get changed, don't you, my angel?"

Patrick reciprocated by kissing Fred gently on the lips and then breaking their embrace.

"What are you going as tonight?" asked Patrick.

"I'm hoping that it's something that will turn you on and have you wanting me to whip you off to bed long before the party has even started," chuckled Fred. "And you? What are you going as, my beautiful man?"

"Nothing too exciting," replied Patrick, opening up his bag, taking out some clothes, and throwing them onto Fred's double bed.

"Are we going to dress together or separately so we don't see each other's character?" asked Fred.

"I don't mind dressing here with you, Fred."

Both men stripped down to their briefs and Fred glanced over at Patrick's heavy bulge and noticed a wet spot on the front.

"Mm, looks like someone has been very excited," he joked, pointing to the wet mark on Patrick's briefs, "And is still very excited, by the size of that bulge."

Patrick blushed and instinctively tried to cover up his erection. However, as he glanced at Fred's half naked body, memories flooded into his mind. He remembered their passionate nights together with Fred's body tight against his, their love-making going on for hours and at all times of the day and night.

"You look so good, Fred, so sexy and I know I want your body tonight. I want you to make love to me as you used to. I want to feel your passion; I want to love every inch of that beautiful body of yours and to wake up in the morning with our arms around each other, our lips locked and our cocks throbbing," said Patrick.

Looking at Patrick's fine body was making Fred lust after it and he wondered if they would ever get dressed for the party.

"Listen, kid, if we don't get dressed now, we never will and I'll be fucking you all night while the others party around us," said Fred rather firmly.

Both men erupted into laughter as they realised that they really did miss each other and were so happy to be back together again.

"I'm going into the bathroom to get dressed," said Fred, picking up his bundle of clothes, leaving Patrick in the bedroom to get dressed.

– – – – –

All the way back to Peter's home, there was silence in the car. It was not until they neared the driveway leading up to the house that the silence was broken.

"Simon, I know you don't have any fancy dress outfit, but don't worry, I'll make a plan," said Keith.

"Where are we going for this fancy dress party?" asked Simon.

"At Peter's Dad's house. It's his birthday."

"Oh, how old is he turning?" asked Simon, naively.

"Sixty-five!" interjected Peter, indignantly. "How old are you, Simon?"

"I turned twenty-one this year."

"I see!" was all that Peter could muster.

At Peter and Keith's home, the partners were busy getting into their fancy dress, while Simon hovered nearby, not knowing what he was supposed to wear. Peter had chosen to wear only a Speedo and a beach towel around his neck and shoulders.

"What's with the Speedo?" asked Simon on seeing Peter.

"I've always had this fantasy of being an Olympic swimmer, ever since I was a little boy, so that's why I'm going like this."

"Aren't you going to be cold?" asked Simon.

"I can always put on one of my Dad's tops if it gets a bit chilly.

Simon laughed nervously.

"What am I supposed to wear?" asked Simon, feeling rather lost.

"I'm afraid I have no idea, Simon. Keith said that he had something in mind for you."

Just then, Keith entered the lounge in his leather outfit. He had on a pair of tightly fitting leather jeans, a leather waistcoat over his bare chest, leather gloves and a black leather cap.

"Wow! Keith, why the leather?" enquired Simon.

"I've always had this passion for leather and I see it as a dominating image too."

"Oh, so you like to dominate?" asked Simon.

"I'm not into whips and chains and such like, but yes, it makes me feel more masculine, manlier and more in control."

Peter never said anything, as he had never seen Keith in leather before. In fact, he did not even know that Keith had any leather clothing and accoutrements.

"You're right, Simon. Wow! I didn't know you had it in you, Keith," said Peter unsure whether to admire his partner or not.

"But what about me?" asked Simon.

"Come with me, Simon," said Keith leading the young man by the arm to the bedroom, with Peter following close behind. "What size waist are you?"

"I don't know. I wear about a medium," he replied.

Keith opened a drawer and pulled out some leather briefs and jockstraps.

"Try those on and see if any fit," commanded Keith.

Simon duly pulled off his jeans and little white briefs that he was wearing. Immediately Keith's attention went to Simon's appendage, to ascertain how big or small he was. As Simon pulled on the first jockstrap, Keith smiled inwardly to himself as the young boy's butt fitted snugly within the straps and the front looked adequately filled. Peter never uttered a word, but watched.

"Here, put this around your neck and see if it fits."

Keith handed Simon a leather studded collar to which was attached a metal chain. Simon placed the collar around his neck, clamped it shut and turned to Keith for approval.

"Yes! That looks good," said Keith, then handing Simon and a leather harness. "Slip that on and then you're ready."

"But what am I supposed to be?" asked a puzzled Simon.

"You're my pet, my boy, my slave. Whatever you want it to be," replied Keith, gleaming with self-satisfaction.

Peter stood there aghast, unsure of what to say, but he could clearly see Keith's enjoyment. In fact, even Simon remained a little puzzled.

Once they got over the sight of each other, Keith led Simon out, much like someone taking their pet dog for a walk might do, and they climbed into the car and headed off towards Fred's house.

– – – – –

Back in Fred's house, Fred came out of the bathroom and stood in front of Patrick.

"What do you think?" asked Fred.

"Mm, very sexy, very sexy indeed," replied Patrick, admiring the tall, well-built man standing in front of him, dressed entirely in the white uniform of a naval Captain. "You look so sexy, Fred. Oh, wow! I think I could strip you right now and have sex with you."

Fred laughed at Patrick's comments, but it made him feel good – he was flattered by his lover's comments.

"Those white pants fit you so snugly and so tight, they emphasize your shapely ass and the jacket fits so tightly across your manly chest... are you sure they're not a small size," quipped Patrick.

'Hey! Don't be rude! However, I'm glad that you like it. But tell me Babe, what are you dressed as?"

"Jeeves, at your service, sir!" replied Patrick, bowing slightly to Fred.

"Jeeves!" exclaimed Fred. "Who's Jeeves?"

"Jeeves, sir," continued Patrick with an artificial British accent, "is a valet, sir."

"And a valet is what, Jeeves?"

"A valet, sir, is a gentleman's personal gentleman."

Fred roared with laughter.

"You're having me on, aren't you? Are you a butler?"

"Not at all, sir, I'm a valet. You see, sir, a valet serves his master, unlike a butler who serves the household, so with that in mind, it is my responsibility to serve you, sir."

Fred liked the sound of that. "So are you telling me that you will do anything that I request?"

"Yes, sir. I am your servant, sir," continued Patrick.

Laughing, Fred added, "You know what Patrick, I think you would do well on stage with your acting."

"Do you like it?" asked Patrick, coming out of his "Jeeves" character and being himself.

Patrick had on a black suit, smart white shirt and a dark tie.

"You actually look like an undertaker. and I wasn't sure if you were fantasizing about death," replied Fred, "but come here, Jeeves, or whatever your name is."

Patrick approached Fred and stood in front of him.

"Kiss me, Jeeves," said Fred, standing to attention like a naval officer.

Patrick had a slight smile on his face as he approached Fred's face.

"This is not a laughing matter, Jeeves," reprimanded Captain Fred.

Patrick stopped smiling, closed his eyes and gently kissed his "Captain".

"That's much better, Jeeves," said Fred, pulling Patrick closer to him. "You do realise that tonight you are all mine and not for anyone else."

"Oh, yes sir," replied Patrick, still adopting his "Jeeves" persona.

They clasped each other, and their kisses were passionate and deep, their hands wandering over each other's body and their breathing getting heavier.

A loud hooting outside of the house broke their embrace and Fred shrugged his shoulders at having to let Patrick loose, as aroused as they both were.

"Damn it!" said Fred, despondently. "I could have stayed with you in my arms all night without being interrupted."

"Me too," came the soft reply from Patrick, who planted a quick kiss on Fred's lips.

The front doorbell rang and Fred knew that this was the start of the party and the end of his passion, for the time being, with Patrick.

"Shall I answer it, sir?" asked Patrick, quickly getting into character again.

"Yes!" laughed Fred. "That would be fun and we can see their reaction."

Patrick moved to the front door and opened it.

"Good evening Gentlemen, welcome to Mr. Summer's residence. Do come in."

Patrick closed the door behind the guests and then turned to face them.

"And who may I say has arrived?" asked Patrick.

"You can tell Fred that Don and Paul have arrived."

Patrick moved back to the lounge, closely followed by Don and Paul.

"A Mr. Don and a Mr. Paul, sir," said Patrick with much aplomb.

"Hi guys," said Fred enthusiastically. "I'm so glad that you could make it, and I had my suspicions about what you would come as, Don," chuckled Fred. So tell me, are you Mr. Universe or what?"

"You got it there straight away, Fred, or dare I say, Captain Fred. It is something that I have always imagined myself as being. How did you guess?"

"It was the skimpy posing briefs that you're wearing. I am actually surprised you managed to find a pair that your big cock could fit into, or have you hidden it somewhere," said Fred, grinning broadly.

"Well, you look very sexy in your white uniform."

"Very becoming," added Paul.

"Thanks guys. Now tell me Paul, what have you come as?"

"I'm a surfer, but Don wouldn't let me bring my surfboard inside so we left it in the truck," replied Paul, adjusting his wet-suit.

"Are you keen on surfing?" asked Fred.

"Ever since I was a kid, I grew up near the sea and always wanted to learn to surf and travel the world, but never got around to doing it," replied Paul.

"Guys, let me introduce you to Patrick here. He's come as Jeeves the butler…"

"… valet!" interrupted Patrick.

"Oops! Sorry! Valet – big difference apparently, so Patrick was telling me. Patrick used to be my partner and then he left to go and teach at another college miles away so we parted ways, but I think he's coming back here so we're hoping to get back together again."

"That sounds great," said Don admiring Fred's tight outfit. "Nice and tight too, I notice," said Don, giving Fred a pat on the ass.

"Can I get you guys something to drink?" asked Fred.

"You know what we like, buddy."

"Okay, Don. Two beers it is then. What about you, Patrick?"

"I think you could make mine a beer as well, thanks Fred. By the way, do you need a hand?"

"Of course he needs a hand. Can't you see that ass is busting out at the back, not to mention the huge bulge that's trying to break free in the front," observed Don.

Patrick and Fred went into the kitchen to get the drinks, leaving Don and Paul alone in the lounge.

"He looks pretty hot in his white naval uniform," remarked Don. "I could go for that, what about you, Paul?"

"Mm, very sexy, but tell me, the other guy, Patrick, is he supposed to be an undertaker with his black suit?"

"I don't know, but he answered the door as though he was the doorman," said Don.

As Fred and Patrick returned with the beers, Don, being the outspoken person that he is, asked Patrick what he was dressed as.

"Fred told you that I'm Jeeves, the valet," answered Patrick.

"So who is Jeeves? Is he an undertaker or something?" enquired Don.

"No, he's like a butler. He is a character in a book written by P.G. Woodhouse."

Both Don and Paul looked very vague and just nodded their heads as if they agreed with what Patrick had just said.

"Have a seat, guys," interrupted Fred, trying to break the uncertainty of the Jeeves mould. "Peter and the others should be here soon, but I have no idea who else he has invited."

Just then, the front doorbell rang once more.

"That could be them now," said Fred, going out to the entrance hall and opening the front door.

"About time. I thought you guys were never coming," said Fred, ushering in Peter, Keith and Simon.

Peter was dressed as a swimmer in his Speedo and seemed to have been shivering from cold on the journey to Fred's house as he had his beach towel wrapped around his shoulders and a pair of tracksuit pants over his Speedo to keep his legs warm.

"What on earth have you come as?" asked Fred when he saw Peter.

"Let me at least get inside and take off my clothes, then you can see," said Peter, shivering somewhat.

Once he was in the warmth of the house, Peter pulled off his track suit pants and stood there in his Speedo and towel around his shoulders.

"I still have no idea, Peter," said his father.

"I'm here as an Olympic swimmer," replied Peter, indignantly. "Couldn't you see that?"

Fred chose not to respond to that and turned instead to Keith.

"And you, Keith? Head to foot in leather, so I am assuming that you have a passion for leather and have always wanted to wear it. Is that it?"

"I'm the controller, the master, the dominator," answered Keith.

Fred raised an eyebrow as he heard the description and immediately he thought back to his conversation with Peter about Keith.

"So, you're into whips and chains and such things?" asked Fred.

"No, not really those things. It just makes me feel manlier and more in control dressing like this."

Then Fred noticed the young man who had spoken to him at the theatre and wondered what he was doing at the party and where Phil was.

"Hi," said Fred, politely. "And what are you dressed as?"

Simon beamed as though he were being presented to a celebrity. "I'm his pet, his boy, his slave. That's what you said wasn't it?" he asked Keith.

"Oh, so you two go together then?" asked Fred, slyly, but watching to see Peter's reaction.

"Well, this should be interesting," muttered Fred, more to himself. "Come through and meet some of the others who are here already."

Fred led the way into the lounge. Keith, Peter and Simon stood in the entrance to the lounge while Don, Paul and Patrick were seated in the lounge. As they entered the lounge, Keith and Peter stopped in their tracks. Peter had a stony look on his face while Keith smiled broadly. These reactions were evident to Fred and he immediately turned to see the reactions of Paul and Don.

"Hi guys," said Keith, crossing over to shake hands with Don and then with Paul. Immediately Fred jumped in by saying," Oh, do you guys know each other?"

"Er, Dad," said Peter, taking Fred to one side and whispering to his father. "These are the nude guys we had around at the house. You remember I told you about it."

"So you did, son," replied Fred, but he was well aware that his son seemed distracted by their presence. "Can I introduce everyone," continued Fred, breaking away from Peter. "This is Simon, who seems to be "attached" to Keith tonight. Simon, this is Don and Paul. They are guys who I have been working with lately."

They all shook hands, but Fred noticed that Peter did not acknowledge either Don or Paul.

"Drinks, guys? We've already got but what can we get for you guys?" asked Fred.

"Whiskey for me if you have," said Keith.

"Beer will be fine for me, thanks," responded Simon.

"Oh Simon, I can see clearly that you're the slave for the night, but why?" asked Patrick.

"I don't know. It was his idea," said Simon, pointing to Keith. "He asked if I wanted to come with him to this party so I said "yes" but then we found I had no clothes to wear so he gave me these to put on. What do you think of them?"

"Oh, very nice and very sexy too," replied Patrick, trying hard not to laugh.

Simon ran a hand over his bulging crotch and then turned around so Patrick could see his little ass and he rubbed that too. Patrick smiled to himself as he thought of the young man's immaturity.

"Tell me, how old you are Simon?" asked Patrick.

"Twenty-one."

"Oh, and what do you do?"

"I'm at university in my last year."

"Hmm, very interesting," replied Patrick.

While Patrick was interrogating young Simon, Keith was ensconced with Don and Paul.

"Peter, do you want to help me get the drinks?" asked Fred, heading off to the kitchen, with Peter following close behind.

In the kitchen, Fred took Peter aside and asked him what was going on between him, Don and Paul. At first, Peter was hesitant but Fred was persistent as he said it was his party and he was not having tension among his guests in his house. Eventually, Peter relinquished and told his father what was concerning him.

"You remember about the nude evening?"

"Yes."

"Well, the two nude friends were Don and Paul. Now, I have nothing against either of them. They're actually very nice guys."

"Yes, I know, I work with both of them."

"Well, the evening was going fine. We had eaten dinner and were sitting around when Keith started telling Don that he would love to take some photos of him. Naturally, Don was keen and so Keith and Don went off to the studio to take photos. They had only gone for about a minute or so when they called for Paul to join them. He got up and went to the studio as well, so I was left in the lounge. I sat there for a while and then I thought I would go and see how the photo shoot was going. As I entered the studio I saw…"

Peter broke off and stood staring ahead of him.

"Go on, son."

"… well, you know there's a table in the studio. Paul was lying on the table with his legs in the air… Keith was … he was fucking Paul… and at the same time… Don was fucking Keith. They didn't see me at first and I was shocked by what I had seen…"

"But son, you had told me that you had a sort of open relationship with Keith, in the sense that, if you both liked someone, you could have a scene with them, so now explain why this was so upsetting to you."

"At no time had I been considered by Keith. He never asked if I was interested in joining in and in fact when he did see me watching, he never asked me to join in, not that I wanted to at that stage."

Fred could see that tears had welled up in Peter's eyes and so he hugged his son warmly.

"Son, these are the things that are sent to try us. If you are going to have an open relationship, you have to realise that somewhere along the line, the rules are going to be bent or broken and that is when the rot starts unless you re-evaluate your relationship. Do you remember me asking you that day you came to visit me, whether you had seen some of the photos that Keith had taken and you said that you hadn't. I saw photos of his on a computer site and they were of naked men, which I do not have a problem with, but there were some that left nothing to the imagination, including some of him in sexual poses with the models. Do you remember me asking you?"

"Yes, Dad."

"It was at that stage that I became concerned for you and your well-being. It wasn't that I was trying to interfere in your relationship; it was that I didn't want you to be hurt. But it looks like you have already been hurt."

"What do I do, Dad?"

"We go back into the lounge with smiles on our faces, we give them their drinks and we enjoy ourselves. Not a word about the incident, but you stay here tonight, even if Keith does not want to stay and do not worry. It will all come right in the end."

"Thanks Dad. I don't know what I'd do without you."

"Hmm, that's what Patrick also says," replied Fred, with a little chuckle. "Peter, I want you to remember one thing. You're a Summers and we do not let people get to us. We always keep that dignity with which we have been born and we will go out there tonight with our heads held high. And one other thing Peter, never walk through life making ugly gashes, never tiptoe through life leaving half-formed impressions. Instead, tread gently, lovingly and purposefully through life, leaving graceful heart-prints. Now, let's take their drinks to them."

Fred and Peter, picked up the drinks, put smiles on their faces and re-entered the lounge where everyone was chatting jovially together. Simon was sitting on the floor at Keith's feet, just as a pet dog might do, looking dejected, while Don and Paul were in deep conversation with Keith. Patrick could sense that something untoward had happened in the kitchen as he could see the red puffiness of Peter's eyes. He glanced towards Fred who simply gave a slight shake of the head as if to say "don't ask".

"Drinks, everyone," announced Fred, handing the drinks around, with the help of Peter, who made sure that he refrained from eye contact with Keith.

"Does everyone have a drink now?" asked Patrick taking the centre of the floor. "I would like to propose a toast to Fred."

Everyone stopped talking and focused their attention on Patrick.

"Fred, you have endured sixty-five wondrous years, some more wondrous than others, but sixty-five years on this earth. I wish you all the happiness you would wish yourself and I hope that the remaining years bring you joy, contentment and a feeling of fulfillment and compassion towards others. May your days be filled with sunshine, love and may you always have friends around you. Finally, Fred, and I know this might not be the correct moment, but I would like to pledge my love to you and if you can love me in your heart as you used to do, that would make me the happiest person in the world. Here is to you. Happy birthday, my love."

There were "cheers" and "happy birthday" shouted out around the lounge, and everyone drank a toast to Fred. Immediately afterwards, Fred took centre stage, as it were.

"Guys, I just want to thank you all for being here tonight. It is always good to have friends around you at times like this, even if it has taken sixty-five years to get you all together. Patrick, thank you for your very kind words and I want to add something to what you said. I would be honored, touched and fulfilled if you were to become a part of my life again. You should never have left in the first place. This will always be your home and I think you know that, and I know that Peter loves you as I do, and he looks up to you as well, so you will always be part of our family as long as you wish. So thanks again and now enjoy yourselves."

The group then burst into song, singing "Happy Birthday" to Fred. As the song was winding down, the front doorbell rang.

"Now who are we expecting?" queried Fred.

"It's probably Brad," answered Peter. "You did invite him, Dad."

"Oh yes, it could be him. Jeeves, would you like to do your little thing again, just for fun?"

"Certainly Sir," replied the very formal and precise Patrick.

As Patrick made his way to the front door, the remainder of those in the lounge remained silent in the hope of hearing who it was. They heard the front door open and then Patrick speak.

"Good evening Sir. May I help you?"

"Yes, is this the home of Fred Summers?" came the question on seeing a butler answer the door.

"It is Sir. How may I help you?"

"I believe there's a party happening here and I was invited."

"You are quite right Sir. However there is a dress code, Sir, and I'm afraid it would appear that there might be some items of clothing missing from your attire."

"I'm sorry, but what are you talking about?"

The others in the lounge were now giggling and laughing in hushed tones at the way that Patrick was leading the visitor on.

"I said that it appeared that you might not fulfill the dress requirements for this party," continued Patrick, with the most serious of faces."You see, Sir, this is a black tie affair and it would appear that you do not prescribe to the requirement."

"Is the owner here?" asked the agitated voice, still unsure if he was at the correct address, even though he had visited Fred before.

"Mr. Summers is in residence, Sir."

"Then I'd like to see him, if you wouldn't mind."

"Certainly Sir," said Patrick, closing the front door and standing there chuckling softly. He rushed back into the lounge. "Should I let him in?"

"I think you're playing your part too well, Jeeves," said Fred, with tears running down his cheeks from laughing. "Let him in."

Patrick returned to the front door, opened it and said, "Mr. Summers will see you now, Sir."

As the visitor walked into the lounge, the entire gathering burst into laughter and welcomed Brad.

"My God! What are you wearing, Brad?" asked Fred, who was still wiping tears away.

"You said we must come dressed as our fantasy and so I have," remarked Brad, looking to see how the others had dressed.

"Yes, that's right," replied Fred, "but please put us out of our misery and tell us who you are fantasizing about."

"You're just going to laugh," said Brad, rather awkwardly.

"No more than what we have already done, but spill the beans and say who you are."

"It's my version of Lady Gaga!" replied Brad.

Naturally, the entire lounge, with the exception of Simon who did not see the funny side to Brad's outfit, erupted into laughter. Even Peter, who had been feeling depressed and miserable up until then, had a grin as wide as the Golden Gate Bridge.

"Why's everyone laughing at him?" asked Simon to Don.

"Have you seen Lady Gaga?"

"Yes, but what's the joke?"

"Have you ever seen Lady Gaga look as ridiculous as this?"

Simon looked long and hard at Brad's appearance, and then shook his head, not so much out of disbelief, but that he still could not see the funny side of it.

To understand the hilarity, it is necessary to describe Brad and his outfit. Brad could be described as a "mini me" to Don. Both Don and Brad were muscular of the gym variety, their only difference being that Don was the tall variety while Brad tended to fall into the vertically handicapped arena in comparison to Don. However, take nothing away from Brad, he was good looking, well built and had a reputation for having sex with anything that moved, provided the moving thing was male and under the age of thirty. Unless of course his age criteria had changed, which it probably had not, although he had made a pass at Fred on his last visit to the house.

On Brad's muscular legs were bright pink tights or leggings and his dainty feet slipped comfortably into scarlet eight-inch platform high heels for which Brad was unaccustomed to walking in them, so he stumbled frequently, when he attempted to walk. Covering his body was a bright yellow sleeveless outfit, which resembled a cross between a lampshade-shaped dress and a pineapple, but without the prickles and atop his head was something that resembled either Carmen Miranda's multi-colored headdress of a fruit salad or a sailing ship at full mast.

"Are you sure you're not Carmen Miranda?" quizzed Patrick.

"Or something out of the ballet "Pineapple Poll"? asked Fred.

The laughter had not subsided since Brad's entrance, but Brad was beginning to see the funny side of his outfit and was beginning to join in with the laughter, but still young Simon remained on the floor with a straight face, not seeing the humor.

"Do you have anything underneath that, should you want to change into something more comfortable?" asked Peter, "because if not I'm sure that Dad has some things that might fit you."

"I think I'll be fine thanks, Peter," replied a smiling Brad.

"Listen guys, there's food on the table over there," said Fred, pointing to the laden dining room table, "so please help yourself as Jeeves is not the butler serving everyone. He only serves me."

"Quite right," reiterated Patrick, "and just remember that I'm the valet and not the butler."

Some of the group got up and started plating up snacks to nibble on, and refreshed their drinks at the same time.

"Hey guys, I was thinking we could do something which might prove interesting if you'd like," stated Fred, calling them together. "I thought we could play something like twenty questions, but reduce it to maybe a maximum of ten."

"On what?" asked Peter.

"On why you chose to come as you did and what your fantasy was," answered Fred. "Is that fine by you?"

There was a stunned silence at first, as they looked at themselves in their various outfits, then they looked at each other, no doubt wondering what the others might make of their fantasies, but eventually Patrick spoke up.

"Sure, that could be fun, and it doesn't have to be taken too seriously. Fred, seeing that you suggested it, why don't you go first?"

"I don't have a problem with that," said Fred, moving into the centre of the lounge so all could see him in his naval uniform.

"You sure cut a handsome Captain," commented Don. "Nice tight, white pants, slim cut jacket that enhances your build, so why did you choose to be a Captain?"

"Right, to answer that, I have to tell you that I had no choice in the uniform – this was the only one available. Next question."

"Why did you choose a naval outfit then?" asked Paul. "What does it symbolize?"

"Right, that's two questions rolled into one, but I'm counting them as two. The uniform symbolizes authority, and I chose it because I love the sea and sailing, as some of you know from when you last visited me and we went sailing along the coast. Any more questions?"

"Yes!" Said Keith, holding onto the chain that was attached to the collar around Simon's neck. "What is your fantasy?"

"I have fantasized being a sailor or someone connected with the sea, but being in a high rank and having someone under me that I can command, but not in a bad way if you understand. It's more in a way that I can have someone under me wanting me as their daddy-like figure, if you know what I mean."

"You mean, like Patrick?" questioned Keith.

Fred turned smiling to Patrick. "Yes, very much like Patrick."

"And do you think that's likely to happen?" continued Keith.

"That's question number six, and its answer is, if Patrick would like that to happen. It is his choice. I will not force myself onto him just to feel satisfied that I have achieved my personal fantasy," replied Fred, drawing admiration from a few of the men, who smiled and nodded in agreement with what he had just said. "Any more questions or are you satisfied with my fantasy?"

They all seemed quite happy with Fred's responses.

"Who's next?" asked Fred.

"I'll go," replied Patrick, "seeing that I was mentioned in your fantasy."

Patrick positioned himself in the centre of the lounge to await the first question.

"When I first saw you, I thought you might be an undertaker," quipped Fred.

"That's not a question," retaliated Patrick. "Stick to questions!"

"Oh, I think I have been reprimanded," said Fred laughing heartily.

"That could put a damper on your fantasy then, Fred, if you upset the co-actor in your fantasy," chided Don.

"Never mind, I'll make it up to him later," retorted Fred, much to everyone's delight.

"So you weren't an undertaker," said Brad, "then why the butler?"

"I'm not a butler; I'm a valet."

"What's the difference?" questioned Brad.

A loud chorus of "Aaghs!" and "Oh no!" greeted Brad from the rest of the lounge.

"Brad, sorry for that, but we've already had that spelt out to us earlier, so let it go and ask another question," suggested Fred.

"Oops, I'm sorry! Right then, why a valet, Patrick?"

"As much as I was married and then divorced, and many people saw me as this macho, butch man, I have another side to me and that is I like to be dominated, but not in the sense that you must tie me down and beat me with whips and chains…"

"… nothing wrong with a bit of whipping," interrupted Don, with glee in his voice.

"Well as I was saying, before being so rudely interrupted by Mr. Universe, I like to please others and by doing that, to serve them in whatever way they wish."

"So you mean that if Fred wants to fuck you, he can?" asked Brad.

"If you put it that way, yes. My function in my fantasy is always to please others more than myself. I suppose that I would get satisfaction from whatever I did for the person, but primarily it is not the pleasure for me, but rather for the man, I serve. Does that answer your question?"

Patrick was greeted by silence, so he resumed his seat next to Fred.

"Come on Brad, I'm dying to hear your fantasy and I think we're all in that boat," said Fred

Brad rose, adjusting his pineapple/lampshade-shaped dress and tottered into the middle of the lounge.

"Before we delve into your fantasy," said Fred, "please explain your outfit to us. What is the significance of the dress, or rather its structure?"

"I think you all know how avant-garde Lady Gaga is in her show stopping appearances. Well, I wanted to emulate her in that respect," said Brad, trying to look demure.

"But what is the significance of the color or the pineapple shape?" resumed Fred.

"No particular reason, simply it was the color of the only dress like it."

"Oh, so you didn't make it?" asked Peter, somewhat sarcastically.

"No, Peter," retorted Brad, indignantly, "I didn't make it."

There was a general guffaw from the crowd in the lounge.

"I like it," said a voice which seemed to have come from the back of beyond.

"Was that you, Simon?" asked Patrick, rather taken aback, as the young man had remained silent throughout most of the evening and, like a pet dog, continued to lie on the floor at the feet of Keith.

"That's interesting, Simon," resumed Patrick. "Why do you like it?"

"Well, I don't know, but I just do. It's like… very feminine… but beautiful… and it's like Lady Gaga would wear."

"Are you a Gaga fan?" enquired Fred, trying to get the young man to open up more and be a part of the group.

"Yes, Sir, I am."

"A little Monster," added Peter.

"That's not very nice, Peter," rebuked Fred.

"No Dad, that's what followers of Lady Gag are called – Little Monsters."

"Oh, I'm sorry, but you seem to forget I'm sixty-five and we oldies don't know such things."

"Can we get back to my questions?" pleaded Brad, trying to get the attention back to him again.

"Oh yes, sorry. Now tell me Brad," asked Patrick, what is your fantasy if you are dressed like Lady Gaga?"

"Funnily enough, it has nothing to do with singing," replied Brad.

"Thank goodness for that," interrupted Don. "I heard Brad singing in the office one morning and fled for fear of being attacked."

"Why attacked?" queried Fred.

"He sounded like a Banshee on the loose." Don smiled apologetically at Brad. "Sorry buddy, but you do."

"Just remember that I'm your boss," censured Brad, and Don adopted a guilty look.

"I have always tried to hide my feminine side," continued Brad, "and I thought this would be a good opportunity to express myself."

"Are you telling us that you're into drag?" questioned Paul, who had been dozing somewhat, probably from the liquor.

"Not into it in the sense that I dress up in women's clothes at home every night, but I do get a kick out of wearing their panties and things."

There were some gasps of surprise and groans from the group on hearing this revelation.

"Brad, when you say "things", what are you specifically referring to?" asked Patrick.

"It's mainly their panties, but I like the feel of their stockings or tights as well."

"I have a question," said Fred…

"… I'm sure my ten questions must be up by now?" said Brad beginning to feel a little like a mouse being forced into an inescapable corner awaiting to be beaten to death.

"One more question, Brad," resumed Fred. "How does this fantasy impact on your sexuality and sexual acts? What I mean is that, when you're wearing women's clothing, do you take on a different role, from what we assume you normally adopt?"

"Are you asking me if I'm a bottom when dressed in female clothing?" asked Brad.

"Yes!" replied Fred.

There was a long, pregnant pause while Brad thought very carefully how to word his answer. He had, after all, a very masculine ego to live up to and most people knew that Brad had always chased the younger boys in order to get them into bed and fuck them Now, to admit to being versatile could damage his image forever, he thought.

"Well… it depends…"

"A simple "yes" or "no" would suffice, Brad," taunted Don, who had sat upright in his seat as Brad's revelation had slowly been divulged.

"As I was saying… it depends on who I'm with…"

"We're not asking you who you are with… we want to know if you are prepared to be fucked when you're in women's clothes or not? Give us an answer, Brad," urged Don.

Brad tried to avoid answering the question and continued to "um" and "argh" in desperation.

"Let me put it to you this way," said Don, with a devilish glint in his eyes. "As you are dressed in female attire tonight, would you be willing to let me to fuck you?"

The group gasped at first and then burst into laughter. A rather indignant Brad could not take the humiliation and fled out of the lounge and the front door was heard to slam shut. Fred immediately got up and followed Brad outside. The rest of the group could not contain themselves and amid chatter and laughter, they began to dissect Brad's fantasies.

Outside, Fred caught up to Brad.

"Brad! Brad! Stop!" called Fred, eventually reaching the fast moving Brad. "Hey buddy, where are you going?"

Fred took hold of Brad's arm and stopped him from running. He put his arms around Brad, who was sobbing softly, and held him fast.

"Hey Brad, don't take this seriously. We all have fantasies and there is no shame among friends to discuss and talk about them. We all have things we would like to be or to have and there is no shame in it. I defy anyone to tell me that they have never had a fantasy at all, because if they did, I would not believe them. Another thing, Brad, there is no harm in being versatile. In fact, I always think that by being versatile, you have the best of both worlds. Even I have desires to be fucked on occasions with the right guy, but that doesn't make me any less a person does it? Of course not! Come back inside, Brad and do not take any notice of what has happened. These are all people who know you and they are not there to ridicule you in any way."

"I don't know if I can, not after having run out like that. They have all seen another side of me that no one has ever seen before."

"Maybe that's a good thing. There might even be some who will respect you more, now. They will be able to acknowledge that other side of you. Tell me, Brad, what are you wearing under that dress?"

"I have on a pair of women's panties under my stockings."

"Well, would you like to slip out of your outfit and put on a pair of my sweat pants and a shirt? I'll bring them out to you and you can get changed and come back inside without your outfit on."

"Would you mind, Fred? I would appreciate that and I know it would make me feel a lot better."

"I'll tell you what, go around to the back of the house and you can sneak into my room from there without anyone seeing you. I'll fetch some clothes and you can get changed there and just leave your clothes as they'll be safe there."

"Thanks Fred. I always knew you were a good guy from the first time I met you in your old house. And, while I am on that, I want to apologize again, for how I behaved that weekend. I know it was a long time ago, but I have never forgotten it. I was screwing around all weekend and I realised that you knew what I was up to, but you remained a thorough gentleman, and I do know I hurt Phil's feelings that weekend and I think that was the cause of our break up."

"Okay, Brad, you head to the back and I'll go and get some clothes for you."

"What are you going to tell them inside?"

"Nothing, except that you are getting changed and will be joining us as soon as you are dressed."

With that, Fred headed back inside the house, while Brad scampered around to the back, found the back entrance and silently made his way into the house and searched for Fred's main bedroom. He found Fred in the bedroom, busily getting substitute clothes for Brad.

"Get out of that junk and put these on," said Fred, handing Brad a pair of his briefs and a pair of sweat pants. "Here's a T-shirt for you as well, Brad."

Brad stripped out of his dress, unrolled his stockings and slipped out of his panties. Fred actually thought Brad looked quite sexy in the panties and stockings but was not about to tell him that, especially after the turmoil that had happened. Brad pulled on the briefs, which fitted him snugly as Brad was a well-hung man, stepped into the sweat pants and then pulled the T-shirt over his head and body. The high-heeled platform shoes were also left in Fred's bedroom and Brad chose to walk about the house, bare footed.

"Right are you ready?" asked Fred.

"Thanks, Fred, you are a genuine buddy," said Brad, hugging Fred warmly.

As they entered the lounge and everyone saw Brad and how he was dressed, they all cheered and applauded him, which obviously made him feel welcomed.

Fred sidled up to Patrick.

"Everything sorted out, Fred?" asked Patrick.

"It was the ridicule that upset him," said Fred.

"But Fred," commented Patrick, "he wasn't really ridiculed. Sure, we all laughed and I think that was mainly because we know Brad's image and this was like a shock or a contradiction. I think the problem is that he has built up this image of himself of being a man, who happens to be a top, and now by exposing himself in his Lady Gaga alter ego outfit, he has done the damage himself. It's not anyone else but Brad, himself."

"I suppose you could be right, Patrick, but I do feel sorry for the guy."

"But why, Fred? Do you feel sorry that he cannot face the reality of his fantasies or do you feel sorry that everyone laughed at him?"

"Maybe it's a bit of both," replied Fred. "Let's just enjoy the rest of the evening."

Fred then turned to the group and said, "No one is to be ridiculed and if you want to laugh, it must be for a valid reason and not simply because you want to make fun of someone else. Now, young Simon, as the newcomer in the room, I think we ought to get to know you and your fantasies."

Simon looked a little bewildered, but he had seen everyone else stand in the centre of the lounge, so he did likewise. The chain attached to his studded dog collar, hung down to the floor and the forlorn look on his face at that moment was beguiling. He looked quite sexy in his black leather jockstrap that enhanced his cute, tight ass and the harness across his chest, emphasized his small Pecs and neat nipples. Keith smiled broadly as he admired the young man.

"Simon, I know that was not your choice of clothes, but do you have a fantasy that you would like to share with us?" enquired Peter.

Fred thought it interesting that Peter had instigated the questioning about Simon.

"I suppose," started Simon, hesitantly, "you could say that I like older men."

There was agreement among most of the guys in the lounge who nodded or muttered softly that they agreed.

"And what about older men, Simon? Is there anything in particular that makes you fantasize about older men?" continued Peter.

"I grew up without a mother – she divorced my father..."

"That seems to be a common trend here tonight," commented Patrick, nudging Fred, who merely laughed and winked at his lover.

"Sorry," said Fred. "Please go on, Simon."

"Well, after my mother left, it was just Dad, me and my older brother. My brother landed up in prison and things changed a little. Dad and I were left on our own and it somehow drew us closer together. We had to support each other, but Dad never remarried or had a girlfriend. I saw him as my role model, being strong and tough and I admired him, both as a father and as the type of man I would like to spend my life with."

Everyone in the lounge had become subdued and silent as young Simon continued his story.

"Go on, Simon," said Fred, who was beginning to get interested in the young man's story.

"Well," said Simon, subconsciously massaging his nipples for all to see, "I left to go to university and I met a few people there of my own age, but one professor... my English professor seemed to take an interest in me and would invite me to his rooms to discuss literature with him. He then ... one night... kissed me and it felt good... an older man like my Dad, kissing me... I wasn't interested in the guys my age. We started seeing each other more often and I began to enjoy his company, but there was something missing... each time I wanted him to make love to me, but he didn't and I didn't know why."

Simon stood there as if in another world, while his audience remained silent. His hands slid down to his pert ass and started rubbing both cheeks, which got many in the lounge very interested.

"Then one evening, I went to his rooms and we did make love... on his desk... and I felt loved and wanted... it just felt right," said Simon with a slight smile on his face, as if re-living the moment.

After a moment, Fred broke the silence by asking Simon, "Does your Dad know about this, and your feelings?"

"Oh yes, I tell him everything. We're very close."

"So what then is your fantasy, Simon?" asked Peter.

"To be made love to by an older man who would want to keep me forever and always love me, then I know I would always be happy, like you guys."

Fred smiled at the child-like innocence of Simon's fantasy.

"Simon, we all wish we could have someone forever and there to be permanent love, but it doesn't always work out like that. However, you must never give up trying to find the right man for you, even if there are hardships along the way. I'm not saying that I'm the ideal model, but

Patrick and I were in love and lived together and then he left to further his career, but now, I'm hoping that we'll be together forever, as you put it."

"Thanks for sharing your story," said Peter, who invited Simon to return to his place on the floor next to Keith. At the same time, Peter glanced at Keith and wondered if in fact this was the right man for him, having listened to Simon's story and then his Dad's comments.

"I think we've had enough of these, Fred," suggested Brad, who had been silent throughout the "interrogations".

"What do you the others feel?" asked Peter.

There was a couple of mumbles, but no one made a committed answer.

"I think, we should have one more," intervened Fred. "Come on Keith, how about you tell us about your fantasy."

Peter glanced at Fred, somewhat bewildered by the tone of his father's voice in inviting Keith to tell his story. Keith rose casually from his seat and wandered rather belligerently towards the centre of the room, but with a smirk on his face. The walk and the look seemed to contradict each other. He stood in the middle of the room, flicked his leather cap to the back of his head, stuck his thumbs into the side pockets of his tight leather jeans and awaited the first question.

"Earlier this evening," said Fred, "when I asked you why the leather, you said that you were the controller, the master and the dominator, I think it was."

"Yes, correct," answered Keith, rather sullenly, as if to manifest the role he wanted to portray.

"Now tell me, who you want to control, dominate and be master over," continued Fred.

"Anyone who wants that sort of lifestyle."

"Oh, so it's not a one-off situation. It's a lifestyle that you really want?" asked Fred.

"Yes, preferably."

"So tell me, or rather, us, do you do all those things in your current relationship?"

Keith threw a glance towards Peter as if to see what his reaction might be. However, Peter sat solemnly staring at Keith without a flicker of a smile, scowl or any other reaction which might alert Keith to Peter's feelings.

"No I don't."

"But it's your fantasy to do those things?"

"Yes."

"So, do you ever get the chance to fulfill those fantasies, Keith – to dominate or be the master?" asked Fred, with a look of anticipated surprise.

"I choose not to answer that question," replied Keith.

There was a hubbub among the rest of the group, demanding an answer.

"I'll tell you the answer to that," said Peter, speaking up angrily. "Yes, he does get the chance to dominate others when he's photographing them, I've seen it."

Keith spun around and glared at Peter.

"Don't talk shit!" he shouted at Peter. "You know nothing."

"If, as you say, I know nothing, then explain the evening that Don and Paul visited us," roared Peter.

Both Don and Paul gulped in horror at the mention of their names.

"You had Paul tied to the table in your studio and you were fucking him, then Don joined in and he fucked you – then who was in control?"

"Cool it, Peter," pleaded Don, "it was just one of those nights when we all felt horny and one thing led to another. There was nothing serious going on."

"You and Paul were not the first ones either," continued Peter, who was now on the verge of either bursting into tears or about to strangle Keith with his bare hands. "Every time he has a model in his studio to "take photos", as he puts it, there are things happening there, but he thinks I don't know about it."

"When and with who have I done anything like that?" questioned

Keith, becoming equally angry that he was being interrogated in front of everyone.

"He would have done that to you too, Simon."

"Why are you picking on Simon?" asked Paul.

"Because Simon is due for a photo session on Friday," said Peter, fighting back the tears. "Why can't you just be honest with me, Keith, and tell me that you were doing all these things with other guys?"

"Because I'm not doing what you suggest, Peter."

"May I interrupt here?" asked Fred, in a calming voice. "I'm not here to defend my son or attack you, Keith. You are both adults and you need to sort out your own problems, but I must admit that I have even seen pictures on the internet posted by you, pictures of you and younger guys with a hard-on and those can only come about when you have been playing around sexually. I think that maybe you both need to have a good and open chat together to iron out whatever is concerning each of you. Remember what the main actor said in the play tonight – something along the lines of "maybe Brad can have his Paulo and I can have my Nick…". Do you remember? Well, you two might need to give and take a little, but be open with each other. If you have certain fantasies, Peter, then you must share them with Keith, and Keith, the same applies to you. It is when you hide things from each other that the trouble starts to form."

The atmosphere in the lounge could be cut with a knife; there was a heavy tension and both Keith and Peter remained subdued and angry.

"I think it's getting late so if you want to go to bed," said Fred, "please make yourselves at home, provided none of you pinch the bed in my room – that's reserved for Patrick and me. There are three other bedrooms and of course you can sleep here in the lounge if you wish. If any of you want to go home, then that's not a problem either."

People started to discuss sleeping arrangements when the front doorbell rang. Fred looked at his watch and wondered who might be visiting at the late hour of one in the morning. He rose from his seat and went to the door. He opened it and there stood a very tall, burly man. Fred looked at his face.

"Evening, may I help you?"

Fred focused on the face, and the man did likewise to Fred.

"Excuse me, Sir," said Fred, "your face looks very familiar but I cannot place you."

"I have the same problem," replied the tall man. "I'm Derek, and I've come to pick up my son."

"Your son?" queried Fred.

"Yes, Simon," answered the man.

Fred looked long and hard at the man and then he slowly began to smile.

"Now it makes sense," said Fred. "You have another son, James who landed up in prison, don't you?"

"Yes, I do," came the answer.

"Derek, I'm Fred. Do you remember when you were a fireman many years back, and I used to visit you?"

"Fred!" exclaimed Derek. "You… and me…"

"Yes, Derek, you and I used to have fun together."

Fred suddenly felt warmth overcome him as his memory flashed back to the days when he and Derek would sneak into bed together and make love until the early hours of the morning and then Fred would sneak home to his wife. Fred immediately burst into laughter at the realization.

"Come in Derek, come in and have a drink," said Fred, ushering Derek into the lounge, having closed the front door.

"Hi Dad," said Simon on seeing his father and going over and giving him a hug.

"Hi Boy, have you been having fun?"

"Yes, Dad, Fred's been very kind to me. Peter," shouted Simon, "Can I get my proper clothes please as I want to get changed."

Simon found Peter and they retrieved his clothes and Simon began to change from his leather outfit into his normal clothes.

"Are you still a firefighter?" asked Fred.

"Not entirely, or should I rather say, no, I'm not. Instead I've become a paramedic," replied Derek. "Still trying to save lives, you know."

"I'm glad about that. You were always good at saving lives," said Fred, with a broad smile. "You sure saved mine. But tell me," asked Fred, "how did you know where to come tonight?"

"Simon sent me a text telling me where he was and to fetch him to take him home"

"I can see that you've brought him up well, Derek. He is a fine young man and you have been a great father as well. Simon did mention tonight that you also were divorced and had to bring up the boys on your own. That makes two of us – maybe it was all the sex we were having together that landed us in the divorce courts," said Fred laughing along with Derek.

"We were actually about to close up for the night and I told the guys they could sleep here or go home, but if you'd like a drink before taking Simon, you're very welcome."

"I'd love to Fred, but I think I should take him home, not that he's a baby. I tend to take care of him, so he's special for his daddy."

"Oh yes, we know how he likes daddies," laughed Fred, "but then I think he gets that from his Dad! Derek, do you stay near here?"

"Yes, about a ten minute drive from your place."

"Well, if you're not staying, will you please come round whenever you'd like and we can catch up on old times. Here, let me give you my mobile number," said Fred, writing it down on a piece of paper for Derek.

"Thanks. I would like that very much, Fred. Just one other thing; are you in a relationship?"

Fred grinned as he remembered those hot nights with Derek and that huge cock that he had and what they did to each other. A glimmer of some inner thrill began to affect his groin area, but then he thought of Patrick and that warm glow started to fade.

"I'm trying to rekindle a relationship, Derek, but that doesn't have to stop you from coming around. Just as a matter of interest, do you have anyone in your life?"

"No, only Simon, but I think deep down he wants his Dad to find a lover. I think we should be off, Fred."

Simon thanked Fred for the lovely evening and both he and Derek left for home. Fred closed the front door with an uplifted heart filled with memories and returned to the lounge where everyone was deciding on who was sleeping where.

"Who was that?" asked Patrick.

"That was Derek, Simon's Dad," said Fred, smiling broadly.

"So what are you smiling about?"

Fred linked arms with Patrick and escorted him out of the lounge towards the bedroom, leaving the others to sort their sleeping arrangements.

"When we're in bed together, I'll tell you all about Derek the fireman and his mighty hose!" laughed Fred.

CHAPTER 10

Patrick snuggled up close to Fred as they lay naked in Fred's queen size bed. The rest of the house was slowly becoming quieter as the other guests sorted out their sleeping arrangements, with Don and Paul sharing a room, Keith sleeping in a room on his own as Peter had chosen to remain sleeping on the sofa in the lounge, and Brad also choosing a room on his own.

"So, tell me about the man at the front door," asked Patrick, resting his head on Fred's chest.

"Right, we have to go far back to when I was still married but I was sneaking off to have a bit of fun, shall we say, before I was caught out. I was having occasional sex with a firefighter. This was before he got married. We would meet at his place where we would climb into his bed and fuck until the early hours of the morning and then I would sneak back into our house and get back into my bed. Well, you remember when you were last at my old house and we had a weekend party and that guy, James, arrived on the doorstep..."

"... yes, I remember him. He landed up in prison didn't he?"

"Yes. Well, he happens to be Simon's older brother, and the man who was at the front door, is their father and so, ergo, Derek."

"So, he's the fuck buddy you had all those years ago? Now where does that put us?"

"What do you mean, where does that put us? I want you in my life and that's final. Not negotiable, so stop worrying about Derek."

"Yes, but now that he's arrived here and knows where you live, does that mean he could be popping in for a quick reminder every now and then?"

Fred chuckled and added, "I told you that you have nothing to worry about, unless of course you want to have a scene with him, in which case, I'll play spectator."

"Don't joke, I'm serious,"

"So am I," answered Fred. "As far as I am concerned, you are part of my life as long as you want to be in it, and if Derek wants to get back into my life, then it will be purely on a friendship basis. If anything sexual arose at any time, I would make sure that you were consulted and part of the moment. What I mean by that is, if you liked Derek sufficiently to say one day that you would not mind having a threesome with him and me, we would discuss the matter and then make a decision about it. Everything in our lives now will be done through consultation. Is that fine with you?"

"Was he the first man you ever had sex with?" enquired Patrick.

"If you must know, yes! And I'll add that he was the first man ever to fuck me – I lost my virginity to Derek."

Patrick was at first somewhat stunned by Fred's revelation, but once he realised that Fred meant what he had said about their love for each other and their relationship, he snuggled even closer to Fred and let a hand drift over the taut, muscular stomach and wander lower down until he felt the tip of Fred's erection.

"And this?" enquired Patrick giving Fred's hard penis a gentle squeeze.

"That's to show that I love you and I need you," replied Fred, rolling over onto Patrick's body and kissing him tenderly.

"Oh, by the way," quipped Patrick, "I recently read an article in which it said that a guy between the ages of say, eighteen and early twenties, takes about three to five minutes to recover from an orgasm. In his late twenties it can take about thirty minutes, while in his forties as much as three to four hours. Well, when he gets to fifty it could take ten to twelve hours but by the time he hits sixty, it might take twenty-four hours."

"And your point being?"

"Well, you've just turned sixty-five, so I was wondering how long it would take you to recover!" said Patrick, with a flirty tone to his voice.

"You just wait until the morning and then tell me how long it took a sixty-five year old man to have sex a couple of times with you, at least," answered Fred, with a tinge of sarcasm in his voice.

Fred could feel how aroused Patrick was and from the passionate kiss, he slid his body down the length of Patrick's body until his mouth reached the throbbing manhood that awaited his mouth.

The groans, moans and movement that emanated from the main bedroom would have kept anyone awake all night, as Fred and Patrick united their love and passion until both men had climaxed together and their breathing had resumed to normal. Their arms remained entwined as did their legs and soon both men were in a dream-like state, happy to be cuddled together.

There were two single beds in Don and Paul's bedroom, but they had chosen to share one bed together. They lay there fast asleep in each other's arms, while in the lounge, Peter had already begun to snore. Keith lay awake on the single bed in his chosen room, thinking about the evening's events and Peter's outburst. His mind wandered to Peter: should he wake him and bring him to the room and they could sleep together? On the other hand, the two men who he had enjoyed sex with lay in the room next door. Brad, however, was someone he had not known before tonight and was not sure what Brad's interests were, other than trying to emulate Lady Gaga.

After much tossing and turning on his bed, Keith got up and

walked quietly from his bedroom and into the lounge. Peter lay curled up in a foetal position on the sofa. Keith stood over him, watching him snore in and breathe out. He stood there for some time, contemplating, and then he quietly moved towards the room in which Don and Paul were sleeping. He stood in the doorway to their room and from the moonlight outside that was flooding into the room, he could see them in the one bed, Don's arms around Paul. From there he moved to the room where Brad was sleeping. He peered in and could see Brad lying naked on top of the bed. Keith moved silently into the room and stood next to the bed, looking down at Brad's muscular naked body. He could see the gentle rise and fall of Brad's chest as he breathed and then his eyes moved down to the flaccid, penis that lay invitingly to one side of Brad's balls. It was thick and cut, the head and shaft moving slightly with each breath that Brad made. Keith was tempted to kneel down and take that thick manhood into his warm mouth, but became unsure of himself. He hesitated, and in doing so, Brad adjusted the position in which he had been lying. He rolled over onto his right side. Keith now had a view of Brad's rounded, yet firm butt. He was tempted once more, but this time to run his hand over Brad's butt. Finally, temptation got the better of Keith. He gently lowered himself onto Brad's bed, who unconsciously shifted over on the bed, allowing Keith more space.

Keith's hand wound around Brad's stomach and he rested his full erection up against Brad's ass crack. Keith felt a slight backward thrust from Brad and so he held his position for a moment. He slowly slid his hand further down Brad's stomach until he felt the thick penis now fully blooded and erect. Keith gently started stroking Brad's penis and at the same time gave gentle thrusts against Brad's ass crack. After a few moments of this, Keith felt Brad's hand slide around, take hold of his hard penis and position it at his ass entrance. Brad then slowly pushed back, impaling himself on Keith's penis.

"Fuck me," whispered Brad, not actually aware who was in the bed with him.

Keith slowly sank his hard manhood into Brad and then started a slow, but rhythmic movement in and out of Brad's butt.

"Oh yes," sighed Brad, "fuck me deeper… give me all your cock… argh yes," groaned Brad, who was now increasing his thrusts onto Keith's cock.

"Do you want my cock, baby?" whispered Keith.

"Yes, yes please. I want all of it," cooed Brad, who by now was well impaled on Keith's hard weapon.

Brad then rolled onto Keith without them losing any contact and ended up sitting on Keith's cock.

"Ride me, baby," whispered Keith.

"Fuck my ass, Keith," said Brad, realizing who it was that was in bed with him. "Fuck me harder," he implored, rising and falling onto the solid flesh and groaning louder each time his ass sank down the full length of Keith's cock.

Keith then placed his hands under Brad's ass to spread it wider and started lifting and dropping him onto his hard cock, causing Brad to bounce and groan even louder, then in one swift movement, Keith flipped Brad over onto his back, got between Brad's legs and lifted them onto his shoulders and continued to sink deeply into Brad's ass. Both men were breathing heavily and both were moaning in unison. Keith's balls were slapping up against Brad's ass and their grunting had now replaced the moans.

A bleary-eyed figure stood in the doorway watching their action. The groaning became heavier and neither Keith nor Brad took much notice of their audience. Their actions became more intense and soon Brad was gasping.

"You're getting me close, Keith."

"Me too, Brad," gasped Keith as he thrust short, quick stabs into Brad's ass.

"Oh fuck!" cried Brad, as the first streams of his seed, flew onto his stomach and chest.

With this, Keith sped up his action, he too was shaking, and his body was shuddering with excitement and passion as he climaxed, filling Brad with load after load of warm cum.

Slowly their breathing subsided and Keith leaned forward and planted a kiss on Brad's lips, followed by a soft, "thank you."

The figure in the doorway remained stationary until Keith had pulled his now subsiding penis out of Brad and lay on the bed next to him. Suddenly the bedroom light went on and Peter stood in the doorway looking at the two exhausted men on the bed. Once he had seen them and they him, he switched off the light and returned to the lounge where he curled up on the sofa once more.

Peter remained lying on the sofa, deep in thought, and noticed that neither Brad nor Keith had left the bedroom, so he assumed that they were going to spend the rest of the night together.

His mind flooded back to the last party that his Dad had enjoyed in his old house, when Brad had ruined his own reputation, if he had much to ruin, when he tried to bed virtually every man at the party. It seemed that this was a repeat of the events of that weekend, but then he thought that he should not place all the blame at Brad's door; after all it takes two to tango, he thought. He then contemplated what his Dad had said earlier, when mentioning the play that they had seen that evening and the lines of the main character, when considering relationships and the idea of give and take. Peter felt that he had been hurt by Keith and could not allow himself the trauma and heartache of Keith playing around with other guys behind his back when they were in a serious relationship. Although he felt hurt, he did not cry or feel the urge to do so; instead he just lay on the sofa, deep in thought.

CHAPTER 11

The following morning, while Peter busied himself in the kitchen making coffee, Patrick lay in the arms of Fred and had a contented smile on his face. Fred, who was also awake, turned to Patrick and saw the smile.

"What are you smiling about, honey?"

"Just thinking," came the reply.

"Thinking that your theory last night might just be a little out?"

Patrick chuckled embarrassedly at Fred's reply.

"Fine, I concede that this particular sixty-five year old man has it in him to have sex at least twice in one night and not need a twenty-four hour respite to get his breath back."

"Or need Viagra or such like to get it up either, twice in one night," said Fred rather proudly.

"You're actually right there," commented Patrick. "If I think about it, not many sixty year plus guys can do it as many times as you can ..."

"... or get it up!" interrupted Fred. "Don't forget that."

"Sure, or get it up," repeated Patrick. "All I can say is that I'm blessed to have you, not only as a loving person but also as a sex machine."

"Well I wouldn't go that far," replied Fred, "after all, machines do tend to give trouble occasionally."

"And Fred doesn't?"

"Not while he can help it. I hear the kettle boiling in the kitchen, so it sounds as if someone is up already."

"Leave them, whoever it is. I'm not letting you escape yet," said Patrick, wrapping his arms around Fred and not allowing him to get out of the bed.

Their lips met once more and soon their bodies were tight up against each other's as they cuddled and kissed each other passionately.

— — — — —

Don and Paul woke up at the same time, both stretched and then both kissed each tenderly.

Don leaned over to Paul and ran his hands over Paul's naked chest.

"Do you fancy a bit of action, Babes?" asked the burly Don.

Paul smiled back, winked and said, "Are you in the mood for some fun?"

"You know me, I'm always in the mood for some hot action, especially with you, you sexy man."

Paul ran his hands over Don's bulging biceps and then onto his rounded, nipples, giving each a gentle tweak with his fingertips.

"Hmm! I can see you want your daddy to deal with you, don't you? When you start playing with my nipples, I know you want it."

"Of course I want it, but I want it from you."

Don maneuvered himself on the bed, pulling Paul up into a crouching position so that he had his back to Don and was kneeling on all fours. Don spread Paul's ass cheeks and admired the small winking eye that watched him. He leaned in closer, and licked the inside of Paul's ass cheeks and then sank a finger into the tight little hole. Paul gasped as he felt the fat finger worm its way into his asshole, then Don began to massage the hole causing Paul to wriggle his ass and push back onto Don's finger.

The two men continued their foreplay until Paul was crying for

Don to penetrate him, which his older and more muscular lover obligingly did for him.

$$- - - - -$$

Peter sat alone at the kitchen counter, drinking his coffee, deep in thought. As he sat there, Keith wandered in, opened the fridge, poured himself a glass of orange juice, closed the fridge door and left the kitchen to go back into the lounge. Not a word passed between them.

Fred, had not gone back to sleep, nor had he let Patrick establish a strangle hold on him, and managed to slip out of bed and made his way into the kitchen.

"Morning, Son, how are you this morning?"

"Fine thanks Dad," replied a subdued Peter.

"Something wrong, Son?"

"Not really, or should I say, not really worth worrying about."

"And that means?"

"Keith is up to his nonsense again, just like Brad was the last time we stayed the weekend at the old house. Do you remember?"

"Oh yes, I remember that well, but what has happened now?"

"I found Keith in bed with Brad last night, or should I say in the early hours of this morning."

"I take it they were having sex?"

"As usual," replied Peter, dejectedly. "I even thought about what you had said last night and what was said in the play, but I cannot compromise my own standards and morals. I believe if you are going to be in a relationship, then it is with that one person only."

"I fully understand, Peter, but have you spoken to Keith about it?"

"No, we haven't spoken."

"Do you want me to talk to him?"

"No Dad, otherwise he'll think that I have to run to you every time there's a problem to be solved."

"Just offered, but I do understand. However, I really think that you must speak to him and either clear the air or come to some solution. You can't go on like this, especially when we know what he does when he's photographing guys. I think that maybe you two should take an early morning walk together and speak your minds."

Peter thought about what his father had said, and it made sense to him. He would speak to Keith and suggest that they take a walk and try to come to some sort of solution, whether it be a break up or a patching up of their relationship. Peter went into the lounge where Keith was sitting just staring into space.

"Keith, I think we need to talk," said Peter softly.

"I've got nothing to say," came the reply.

"Keith, I know that when you know that you've done something wrong, you always say that you've got nothing to say or you don't want to talk, but I think we need to talk this time. Can we at least go for a walk and try to sort this problem out?"

"I don't have a problem," came the curt reply.

"It's no good trying to deny it, we do have a problem and this time I'm not going to leave it like I usually do, hoping that it will blow over."

"I told you I have nothing to say to you."

"Well, I'm not leaving this lounge until we speak and if others come in and hear our discussion because you don't want to take a walk outside where other can't hear us, then so be it."

"God! You're such a pain!" blurted Keith getting off the sofa and heading to the front door, which he opened, stormed out and slammed the door behind him.

Peter quickly followed him out and ran after Keith.

"Keith!" shouted Peter. "Stop!"

Keith kept striding towards the beach, with Peter hurrying after him, still shouting for him to stop. Eventually Keith came to a stop on the edge of the sandy beach. He sat down on the sand and wrapped his arms around his knees, clutching them to his chest. Peter reached him and sat down on the sand next to Keith. Neither said a word.

The waves seemed to sense something was about to happen, because as Peter sat down, a couple of waves crashed loudly onto the shoreline. The beach itself was deserted, except for the two men.

Eventually Peter decided to break the impasse and spoke to Keith.

"Keith, I know we've had our problems before and I know we've never sat down and spoken about them, but I think it's time that we did."

There was no verbal reaction from Keith.

"Please tell me why you went into Brad's room last night and had sex with him? You know you could have had sex with me."

The only sound was the ebb and flow of the waves breaking on the shoreline.

"Why did you have sex with Brad?"

No response.

"Keith, I'm talking to you. Will you at least give me an answer as to why you decided to fuck Brad last night," said Peter, raising his voice.

"Because I wanted to," was the abrupt answer. "Satisfied?"

"Not really. Can you tell me why you are not interested in having sex with me anymore? What have I done to deserve being neglected like this? You never even want to touch me, but I see how you fawn over young boys and the guys you take photos of in the studio. Even Brad, whom you have never seen or met before, you are into bed with him at the drop of a hat. Why?"

Keith remained staring at the waves breaking but chose to remain silent.

"Had you and Brad arranged this before going to bed? I wouldn't put it past you."

"Nothing was arranged. It was spontaneous. I went into his room and he looked so inviting lying there naked and I couldn't control myself and so I climbed into bed with him, and that's the truth."

"So you're telling me that it was something beyond your control? Does that also apply to all the other incidents? I doubt it."

Peter remained silent for a moment and then continued as he had an instant to reflect on Keith's behavior.

"When those boys and men arrive to be photographed, are you telling me that when you have sex with them it's also because you have no control? If that is the case then I suggest you see a doctor. Better still see a psychiatrist. I think you are a sex addict and it's just that you can't get enough sex that drives you to want to bed other guys instead of me."

Keith hung his head and rested it on his knees. He remained stoic and refrained from speaking.

Peter stood up and dusted off the excess sand from himself.

"Keith, I think it would be better if you packed your bags and moved out. In fact, I don't even think you should consider waiting until the end of the month. As everything that is in our home belongs to me, you can move out right now. Pack your clothes, take your photographic equipment and go. I do not really care where you go. You can move in with Brad for all I care. Maybe you might be able to share Don and Paul's home, seeing that you like threesomes with them. Speak to them when you get back to the house, but I'm finished with you and your nonsense. I'm tired of being using others for your own sexual satisfaction and I'm not going to put up with it anymore."

Peter did not wait for a response or a plea from Keith, but turned on his heels and headed back to Fred's house. As he stormed into the house, through the back door, Fred was waiting in the kitchen. He could see from the expression on Peter's face that something untoward had happened.

"Do you want to talk, Peter?"

"Not now, Dad. Maybe later," said Peter continuing into the bedroom and beginning to pack Keith's clothes into a bag.

As he packed Keith's clothing, he kept mulling over the idea of once more living on his own. Was he destined to a life of solitude? What would his friends say? That he was unable to keep a relationship? Questions kept flooding his mind and he stopped at one point, looked at the suitcase and wondered if he was doing the right thing about getting rid of Keith.

Fred came to the bedroom doorway and stood there, peering in. Peter saw his father as he was considering his actions.

"Am I doing the right thing, Dad?"

"Son, only you know," said Fred, entering the bedroom and sitting on the bed to watch his son continue packing. "I know what I would do if it were me, but it isn't me, so I'm not about to offer you my advice."

Peter looked long and hard into his Dad's eyes and then said, "You'd kick him out, wouldn't you?"

Fred smiled and nodded his head.

"So, you don't think I'm doing the wrong thing then?"

"Personally, I felt you should have done it a long time ago, but I have always told you from a child, that I would not interfere in your decisions in life. I am willing to offer advice should you ask for it, but in this case, you need to make the decision. After all, you are no longer a child. You are a man and as a man, you have the ability to decide on your future."

"I know, Dad, and I appreciate what you have taught me over the years, but when it comes to love matters, I really don't have much experience there."

"Son, let's put it this way," said Fred, chuckling a little, "when it comes to love I might know more than you because I've been around longer than you, but when it comes to men, you probably could teach me a thing or two about them."

Peter joined in the chuckling. This laughter tended to break the tension that had arisen in Peter, but it had not broken his resolve. He was determined to carry out his promise of breaking up his relationship with Keith. As Fred sat on the bed chuckling with Peter, Patrick came to the doorway.

"I think Keith is coming in, Peter," said Patrick, which alerted Fred, who rose from the bed and together with Patrick went out and back to the kitchen.

"What's the decision?" asked Patrick, once they were out of

earshot.

"It seems that Peter's made up his mind about this and he's kicking Keith out," said Fred, shrugging his shoulders as he said it.

"I don't blame him. I just found there was something odd about the guy. I couldn't put my finger on it, but if it's going to make Peter happier without him, then that makes me happy too."

As they sat discussing the events leading up to Peter's outburst with Keith, Don and Paul came into the kitchen all bleary-eyed.

"Morning, you two," said a cheery Fred. "Coffee for anyone?"

"Mm, please," replied Don, trying to remove the sleep from his eyes, "and for Paul, I think."

"I'll get it, Fred," said Patrick, busying himself at the coffee percolator.

"Was I dreaming or did I hear some shouting earlier?" asked Don.

"Shouting?" queried Fred. "I didn't hear any shouting."

"Well, maybe not shouting but raised voices," continued Don, who had arrived in the kitchen only in his miniscule posing briefs, and was now busy scratching his balls through the Lycra material.

Both Fred and Patrick eyed the heavy bulge in the front of Don's briefs as it got fumbled, stretched, scratched and then finally, a hand dug into the briefs and Don must have given his cock a sort of wake up squeeze.

"I think it might have been Keith and Peter," replied Fred, nonchalantly, not really wanting to elaborate on what had happened.

"Oh, a lover's tiff, no doubt," said Don, now busily scratching his ass.

Again, Patrick and Fred watched this animalistic routine before them and fought hard not to laugh at Don's antics. All throughout this, Paul had stood motionless in his boxer shorts, also watching Don. It was almost becoming a one-man show in the kitchen. As Don continued scratching and manipulating his heavy penis and balls, Keith entered the kitchen carrying his suitcase.

"Could I see you for a minute, please Fred?" asked Keith, a little subdued.

Both Fred and Keith went out the back, and were seen talking to each other. The others remained in the kitchen, quiet, in the hope of hearing something being said, but to no avail. Just then, Peter entered the kitchen, saw the others in a tableau effect, all still and stationary, and then returned to the bedroom. They saw Keith leave Fred and go to his car, throw the suitcase onto the back seat, climb in, start the car and head off.

Fred re-entered the kitchen and was almost attacked by the others to find out what had been said.

Fred shook his head in disbelief that they were like vultures, waiting to dig into the pickings that had been left behind.

"So! What was his story?" asked Don, with excited enthusiasm.

"He just said that he would be leaving Peter and thanked me for the evening," replied Fred, casually.

"Is that all?" questioned Don. "Nothing else?"

"Sorry to disappoint you guys, but there's nothing else to say."

"Nothing!" exclaimed Don, "but we could see you talking, quite a lot too."

"Listen guys, this is between Keith and Peter and it should not be part of our business, so don't even try to get me to say more, because I won't," replied Fred. "Case closed!"

There was obvious disappointment on all their faces, but Fred was a man of his word and he stuck to it.

As they sat in the kitchen, disillusioned by what they saw as Fred's lack of cooperation, Brad marched into the kitchen, looking sprightly and with a spring in his step and wearing a towel wrapped around his waist.

"Morning all," he said happily.

"Morning," replied the others in varying shades of enthusiasm and excitement, or lack thereof.

"What's the matter with some of you, are you hung over from last night?"

"No," answered Paul. "Keith's just left."

"Oh, that's too bad. I was hoping to say cheers to him and thank him," said Brad.

"For what?" asked Paul.

"Last night. Or should I say, the early hours of this morning," replied Brad with a smile that spread from ear to ear.

"Why, what happened last night?" enquired Don, with a perplexed look on his face.

"Well, shall we say we had some fun," giggled Brad. "You remember what he said about his fantasies last night, well he got to fulfill them," he continued smugly.

"I don't understand, Brad?" said Don.

Fred decided to interrupt before things go out of hand, especially as he realised that Brad had no idea that Keith and Peter had broken up and that Keith had actually been packed off by Peter.

"Um, Brad I think you and I need to have a little chat, if you don't mind. Come with me," said Fred, taking Brad by the arm and leading him towards Fred's main bedroom.

"By the way," said Brad as he was being led to Fred's bedroom. "Do you think you could lend me something to wear, other than Lady Gaga's outfit?"

"Sure," replied Fred, as they disappeared into the bedroom.

"What's going on now?" questioned Don.

"I think that Brad was party to something last night," suggested Patrick, as politely as he could.

"Like what?" asked Paul.

"They had sex together," replied Patrick, eventually.

"You mean Keith and Brad?" asked Don.

Patrick nodded his head in the affirmative.

"Now it makes sense to me," resumed Don, "about him fulfilling his fantasy. He wanted to control and dominate someone and that someone happened to be Brad – maybe that is also why Brad looks so happy this morning."

"But what about Peter?" asked Paul. "How is he taking it?"

"Apparently it was Peter who caught them at it and he went after Keith and told him he wanted nothing more to do with him."

"Peter told him that?" asked Don. "I never expected that of Peter. He always seems such a mild mannered, quiet sort of person."

"Well there's a lesson to be learnt there, Don. Don't judge a book by its cover."

"You're absolutely right, there, Patrick," said Peter, as he entered the kitchen.

"Are you all right, Peter?" asked Paul, giving him a hug.

"I'm fine now, thanks Paul. I think I should also thank you and Don, because had it not really been for you two guys coming to our nude evening and me seeing what happened that night, and of course, Dad pointing certain things out to me that had appeared online, I would have been blind to all his goings on."

"Listen Peter, we're sorry about what happened at your place that night, we truly are but we got the impression that both you and Keith were into sharing like that, if you know what I mean," said Don, offering a type of apology.

"I think I also owe you an apology, Peter," said Brad, as he re-entered the kitchen with Fred. "I must confess that I was asleep at the time and only woke up when Keith was already busy with me."

"Brad, I'm not blaming you just as I'm not blaming Don and Paul. You could be seen merely as pawns in Keith's little games. I realised that he wasn't happy with just one person in his life and he needed his sexual urges fed somewhere else."

"Much like me, I'm afraid," suggested Brad. "That's why I cannot have a relationship as I want more, not more people in the relationship, but more sex. I think you and your Dad are well aware of my sexual urges."

"Oh yes," replied Fred, putting an arm around Brad's shoulders. "Brad, we know that deep down you're not bad…"

"… Gee thanks!"

"But we know you and you're open about it. You see, Keith was never open about his desires and now it has hurt Peter, having found out. Perhaps had he been more open to Peter, things might have been different, although I personally doubt it, knowing Peter as I do. The same applied to you Don, and your relationship with Paul. I had no idea that you were partners until you opened up to me and how your sex life panned out, and then I began to understand how you might "play around" with other guys."

Don began to understand and so did Brad.

"Personally, I don't blame Peter, not just because he's my son," continued Fred, "but I hope that this has been a learning curve for Peter, and any others who might be in the same situation. It is not that I have a hatred of Keith; it is just that I do not approve of people using others to their own advantage. If you're going into a relationship you need to be completely open right from the start, if you hope that the relationship will last."

"Good advice," said Don, nodding in agreement, as Fred gave forth his theory of love and relationships.

"I sincerely hope that this incident is not going to ruin our relationship, Fred?" stated Brad, "as you are a very good friend, and I'm impressed with your work ethics."

"Brad, you have nothing to fear," replied Fred. "It wasn't my relationship that ended and you hadn't slept with my boyfriend, or at least I don't think you have."

"Trust me I haven't... yet!"

Both men laughed heartily and Patrick joined in once the realization set in that they were talking about him.

"And you are not likely to," said Fred, sounding like a father reprimanding his child. "I'm very grateful that you offered me that job and I'm going to ask you another favor. Is there a possibility that Patrick can join as my apprentice?"

"Your apprentice?" questioned Patrick, rather indignantly.

"Do you want the job or not?" asked Fred.

"Of course," replied Patrick.

"Then you're my apprentice and remember that I'm the boss," said Fred, now reprimanding his lover.

"No, no, no, Fred! I am the boss, so just remember that," commented Brad, "and just remember who hires and fires!"

Fred and Patrick both laughed at Brad's correction, but both realised that Brad was right; he was the boss and they depended on him for their jobs, so they would have to play ball, so to speak.

"If you're the boss, Brad, and there I agree with you that you are, I think we need to draw up a new contract in which it states that the boss is not allowed to fraternize with the staff," said Fred.

Don and Paul both applauded loudly in agreement.

"If that is the case, then he can't try to bed either of us as well," said Don, gleefully.

"Not a problem," said Brad, confidently.

"You mean that?" asked Fred.

"Of course. No fraternizing with staff during working hours," added Brad.

"No, no! That's not acceptable," said Don, realizing how Brad had manipulated the agreement.

"Don, I'm more than willing to put it into the contracts that I will not fraternize during working hours – seeing that I pay your wages – but after hours, the contract is null and void."

Paul suddenly woke up to the fact that Brad could have sex with anyone of his staff after working hours and this appealed to him and he saw the funny side of it.

"Guys," said Fred, "you're welcome to stay on for the day if you haven't got work to go to or that you're unemployed, but if you have to get to work, then I suggest you shower and head off. I take it, Don, that we don't have any work today?"

"As far as I'm aware, we're free today. Is that so, Boss?" he said, turning to Brad.

"I'm sure that if the boss, as you put it, is taking the day off, then I'm sure that the workers can also have the day off."

"Three cheers for the boss," joked Don.

Nobody responded, but they did breathe a sigh of relief that they could have the day off.

"Does that mean that I can go back to bed, Fred?" enquired Brad.

"I'm sure that you can, Boss, but don't expect breakfast in bed. This isn't a hotel."

Brad wandered back to his room and shouted as he left, "If any workers want to join me, they are most welcome!"

CHAPTER 12

Peter, Fred and Patrick sat out in the garden, listening to the waves breaking on the shore, enjoying cups of coffee.

"Do you think I did the right thing, Dad?"

"Peter, only you know the answer to that question. Neither Patrick nor I can honestly give you a definitive answer. How do you feel inside, in your heart?"

"I'm a little mixed up to tell the truth. A part of me already realises that my home will be empty when I get back there, but another side of me seems to have breathed a sigh of relief that I don't have to worry as to whether Keith is up to anything or not."

"Son, you don't have to worry, as I'm sure the right person will come along and you'll be happy just as Patrick and I are."

"You mean I must wait until I've turned sixty-five before I find Mr. Right?" asked Peter, sarcastically.

"Of course not!"

"I'm only joking, Dad. I meant to ask you last night. Who Simon had gone home with as I saw an elderly man here."

Fred laughed at the mention of the 'elderly man'.

"Peter, if you think that man was 'elderly', as you call him, then you must be categorizing me as well."

"Why?"

"He's about my age," replied Fred, with a sly grin. "It was actually Simon's Dad."

"Oh, I wasn't aware of that," said Peter.

Fred and Patrick exchanged glances to each other. Patrick was waiting to see if Peter pursued his line of questioning, and how Fred was going to respond to them.

"Son, it's only fair that I tell you about Simon's Dad, as I'm the one who advocated that there should be communication in a relationship. I'm sure you remember me telling you about the fun I used to have when your mother and I were still married? How I sneaked out at night and met up with this firefighter and we would spend the night together? Do you remember me telling you?"

"Yes, I sure do. Quite a horny man, eh?"

"Well, Simon's Dad was the fireman."

Fred waited for that to sink in and to see Peter's reaction.

"Well, it's nice that you guys have met up again," said Peter.

That was not quite what Fred was expecting. He thought Peter might be angry or worse still, he might assume that Fred was going to 'dump' Patrick for Simon's Dad.

"Are you going to see him again, Dad?"

"If you mean am I going to start up my nightly trips to Derek, that's his name, no, it's not going to happen as I have Patrick in my life now."

"Oh! But will you see him again? I mean like have a drink together?"

"I would very much like to have a drink with him, but this time I want Patrick to meet him and for the three of us to get to know each other better."

"How do you feel, Patrick?" asked Peter.

"I would be very happy to meet your Dad's friend. After all, you cannot have a relationship like they had back then and now pretend that it never happened."

Patrick was so close to mentioning Fred having lost his virginity to Derek, but he caught himself just in time and did not mention it to Peter.

"Often," continued Patrick, "when two people meet for the very first time, they develop an immediate connection and sometimes that connection stays with them for life. In this case, I think that Derek and you Dad had that connection and although your Dad has promised to spend the rest of his life with me, and I with him, there is no reason why he cannot meet up with Derek again."

He hoped that he had made Peter understand both his and Fred's position.

"Wouldn't you be jealous of their friendship?" asked Peter.

"Not at all," answered Patrick. "Let me ask you a question. Are you jealous of me being with your Dad?"

"No, not at all!"

"Why not?" persevered Patrick.

"Well, I suppose because your love and my love for him are different."

"Exactly, Peter. I love your Dad as a sexual partner who I want to spend the rest of my life with, but you love him as a father who will be there when you need him. It's the same with Derek. I assume that your Dad will befriend him and maybe love him as a friend but not a sexual partner. Often people cannot distinguish different forms of love. I know of so many men who become possessive of their partners simply because the partner has feelings of deep friendship for another person, even though there is no sexual connection between them. Yes, I acknowledge that your Dad and Derek had sex together many years ago, but that has passed and now they can be close and good friends and I can love both of them if I choose; I can love Derek as a good friend and I can love your Dad as my partner for life. Now do you understand?"

Peter sat silently, while Fred took hold of Patrick's hand and gave it a gentle squeeze.

"That was so beautifully put, my darling," whispered Fred. "I know that I have made the right choice in you. You are not only a beautiful man outside; you are also beautiful inside too. In fact, I think you would have made a great father."

Fred leaned across and kissed Patrick gently on the lips.

"Peter, treat each day as if there is a tomorrow; whether it comes or not, we never know, but it's always good to think of tomorrow, and should tomorrow arrive, there is no doubt it will be different from today, and with it will come different emotions, different ideas and different people. In other words, Son, take what life dishes out to you and make the most of it. As you are well aware, life is never a smooth ride to some distant destination. It is filled with rough roads, potholes, mountains to climb and river to cross, and you can either succumb to those obstacles or overcome them – the choice is yours in life."

Peter sat listening intently to his father's words. He realised just how wise his sixty-five year old dad was and he respected that wisdom.

Don, who had been inside with Paul, and had dressed, came out to the back where Fred was talking to Patrick and Peter.

"Sorry to trouble you guys, but there's someone to see you, Fred. He said he'd like to see you alone."

"Who is it?" asked Fred.

"I don't know his name but I saw him here last night. He's the guy who took Simon off with him."

"Oh, that can only be Derek, Simon's Dad," answered Fred.

"Visiting all ready," said Patrick, a little indignantly.

"I'm sure it's nothing like you think, Patrick, but let me go and see what he wants," replied Fred, leaving the men outside to continue chatting.

Fred went into the lounge and found Derek standing waiting for him, looking rather solemn.

"Hi Derek, nice to see you again. Did Simon leave something

behind last night?"

"No, Fred, and I'm not here for a social visit either."

"Oh, I hope we didn't disturb the neighbors last night and they've laid a charge against us, have they?"

"No, not as far as I know. I was called to a road traffic accident a couple of hours ago, told Simon about it when he got home, realised it was Keith and I had to come straight over."

"What happened?" asked Fred, shocked by the revelation.

"We're not sure exactly how it happened, but the car definitely hit a tree. But as I say, we don't know if he had to swerve to avoid something like an on-coming car or not."

"Is he in hospital?" asked Fred.

"No, I'm afraid he didn't make it," answered Derek.

"You mean…"

"… yes, I'm afraid he was killed instantly."

Fred gasped in shock, covering his mouth with his hands, as if to stifle the cry.

"Oh, my God! I'll have to tell Peter, and I have no idea how he'll take it."

"If you'd like me to stay a while to see that Peter's okay, I'll gladly do that for you, Fred."

"Thanks, Derek. I really appreciate your kindness, but I must think how to tell him. You see they had a bust up last night and Peter told Keith to get out of his life, and I'm sure that he'll feel guilty about what has happened now."

"Would you like me to talk to him, Fred?" asked Derek.

"I honestly don't know. Maybe we could both be there, if you wouldn't mind, just in case he needs something to calm him down."

"Of course I'll be there for you, Fred."

Derek remained in the lounge while Fred went out to call Peter inside, but also told the other two that he wanted to speak to Peter privately. Peter accompanied Fred into the lounge where a solemn Derek was waiting.

"Have a seat, Son," said Fred, ushering Peter to the sofa and then sitting beside him. "You haven't met Derek officially, have you? This is Simon's Dad and a very good friend of mine too."

Peter immediately knew what Fred meant by "a very good friend" so he wasn't at all surprised.

"Peter, I'm afraid that Derek has brought us some bad news."

Peter looked startled by the statement and glanced from his Dad to Derek and back to his Dad.

"What news?" questioned Peter, still a little bewildered.

"There was an accident last night or in the early hours of this morning," continued Fred, "and it involved Keith."

"Is he all right?" asked Peter, urgently.

"Peter, I'm afraid not," replied a calm Fred. "No one seems to know what happened but his car hit a tree."

"Is he in hospital, Dad?"

"I'm afraid not, Son. Keith didn't make it."

"What!" gasped Peter, who immediately burst into tears at the realization of what had happened. "That's my fault," cried Peter, sobbing loudly. "I sent him away and it happened because of me!"

"No, no Peter. It was not your fault. We don't know if he swerved to avoid another car or an animal, but he didn't kill himself on purpose. It was an accident and it was just very unfortunate that his car skidded and collided with the tree."

"Would he have suffered, do you think?"

"I don't think so, Peter," replied Derek. "It probably would have been instantaneous death. He may not have even felt anything. I doubt he even saw it as it was dark."

Peter sobbed uncontrollably and both Fred and Derek tried their best to console him.

"Son, why don't you go and lie down in my room. Derek will give you something to make you sleep, but just remember that it was not your fault."

Fred helped Peter to his feet and took him to his bedroom while Derek got a glass of water and took it, along with some tablets, to Peter in the bedroom. Fred sat on the bed next to Peter as he took the tablets and then lay down on the bed, still sobbing.

"Do you want me to stay, Fred?" asked Derek.

Fred shook his head. "I don't think so, Derek. I think he'll be fine once the tablets take effect, but thank you so much. We really do appreciate your kindness in letting us know."

"Don't mention it, Fred. If you need anything at all, even in the night, please don't hesitate to call me."

"Thanks, Derek."

"I'll see myself out," continued Derek. "Do you want me to say anything to the others on my way out?"

"If you wouldn't mind, Derek, but ask them not to come to my room as I want Peter to get some sleep now."

Derek left the room and made his way outside to Patrick, Don and Paul. He gave them the bad news, which shocked all three of them and relayed Fred's message which they accepted. Derek then said that he was leaving, but Patrick insisted that he would see Derek out.

"Derek," said Patrick with warmth in his voice. "Thank you so much for all that you have done for Fred. He has told me all about you and how close you two guys were and I just want you to know that I hold no jealously against you and I warmly accept you into our lives, and in fact, I really would like to get to know you better. Please take this as an informal invitation that whenever you can, please come and have dinner with us. Bring Simon too if you'd like, he's also most welcome here."

"Thanks Patrick, I appreciate your gesture and I would very much like to get to know you as well, after all I think we both love him in our own different ways; you as his lover and me as his friend, but let's see how things go today and wait for tomorrow. At the moment, my concern would be for Peter, so please be there for both him and Fred and if you need anything, I told Fred to contact me any time of the day or night."

Patrick instinctively took Derek into his arms and hugged him, laying his head on Derek's broad shoulder. As the two men hugged each other, warmth seemed to exude from the one to the other and vice versa. They remained like this for quite some time and then broke free.

"Tomorrow!" said Patrick.

"Tomorrow!" replied Derek.

Derek left and Patrick went back to where Don and Paul were, who were still reeling in shock.

"I know that Peter and Keith had their differences," said Paul, "but this is traumatic. You don't expect these things to happen like that."

"It's life, Paul, you never know when it's your time to go," said Don, putting an arm around Paul's shoulders to comfort him.

"Apparently it was sudden," said Patrick, when he joined them, "so I'm assuming that Keith probably didn't know what hit him."

"Can I make you guys some tea or coffee?" offered Paul.

There was a chorus of acceptance.

"I think I should go and see if Brad is awake and tell him the news," suggested Don. "Remember he went back to bed so he won't have any knowledge of what has happened."

"Good idea, Don," replied Paul, "I think he should be informed as it was Keith who spent the night with him, wasn't it?"

Don excused himself and headed to the bedroom in which Brad was sleeping. He entered to find Brad still very much asleep. He shook him gently to awaken him without giving him a fright.

"Brad," whispered Don, close to Brad's face. "Wake up, I need to speak to you."

Brad stirred slightly and then rolled over onto his right side, facing away from Don. As Brad was sleeping on top of the bed and not under any duvet, Don could see the firm, rounded butt, waiting to be kissed, stroked or even slapped! He was tempted to do all three, but thought it might be a little inappropriate under the circumstances. Instead, he placed a hand on Brad's left hip and shook it gently. Brad grunted and turned to see who was behind him.

"Hi Don," said a sleepy Brad, shifting further onto the bed as if to allow Don to lie next to him.

"Do you want to hop on next to me?" enquired Brad, patting the spot next to him.

"No thanks, Brad, as tempting as it is, but I need to speak to you. Are you properly awake?"

"Yes, why?"

"Then sit up and listen to me carefully."

Don waited as Brad rearranged the pillows as a back support then he sat up against the headboard.

"So, what do you want to tell me?"

"Brad, Keith was involved in a car accident and unfortunately he didn't make it."

Brad looked stunned.

"You mean he's dead?"

"Yes, Brad. He apparently died instantly."

"What happened?" asked Brad, still in shock.

"Nobody knows for sure, but his car struck a tree and he was killed outright."

"That's awful. Does Peter know?"

"Simon's Dad came around and told Fred who then passed on the message to Peter. He was in a serious state of shock so they gave him some tablets to take to make him drowsy and so far as I know, he's still sleeping."

"Have you any idea who might be arranging the funeral and when it will be held?" asked Brad, very much awake now.

"No idea, but I'm sure that Fred will have all the details for us sooner or later," replied Don. "Come on, Brad, I think you should get up and come and have some coffee with us in the kitchen."

Brad hauled himself from the bed and together, with Don, they made their way into the kitchen where they found Fred.

"How's Peter?" asked Brad, on seeing Fred.

"He's sleeping, thank goodness, Brad. I imagined that although they had a bust up, he might take the news badly and he did. I presume that one of the others has explained what happened?"

"Yes. To some degree, but does anyone know why or what caused him to crash?"

"No one seems to know the details," said Fred, solemnly, "but whatever they were, the fact remains that Keith is no longer with us and I think we need to think of the positive and good things he did in his life. I know how easy it is to remember the negative aspects, and we all do that, but we really have to focus on the fact that he did bring happiness to others."

"Sure, but I think there were so many others who also benefitted by his love and friendship, including Peter," retorted Brad.

"I'm sorry, Brad, I shouldn't have picked on you like that."

"It's not a problem, Fred; it's just that we must remember that Keith brought happiness to a lot of men, not just Peter and me."

At that moment, Fred's mobile phone rang.

"Fred Summers speaking. Oh, hi Derek, this is a nice surprise, what can I do for you?"

"Hi Fred," said Derek into the telephone, "I just wanted to let you know that Keith's funeral is tomorrow at 10:30am."

"So soon," replied Fred. "I don't mean time wise, but day wise."

"Keith apparently was Jewish and as you may or may not know, they like to bury their loved ones quickly, much like the Muslims," continued Derek.

"Actually I did not know he was Jewish, but I'll tell the others and we can all meet at the cemetery tomorrow. Are you going to the funeral?"

"Yes, Simon wants to go, so I said I would accompany him. Then I'll see you there?"

"Sure thing."

"By the way, how is Peter?"

"Sleeping, so I think that's a good sign, but I'll keep an eye on him. Thanks again Derek. Bye."

Fred switched off his phone and relayed the message to the others around him.

A Boner Book

CHAPTER 13

So often one conjures up pictures of funerals taking place on rain-soaked days with everyone dressed in black and carrying black umbrellas. There is always a sense of gloom and doom, and quite rightly, but today it seemed somewhat different. Admittedly, there was the feeling of gloom and doom, which was natural as it involved the loss of one of the 'group', so to speak. However, the manner in which the attendees dressed when they arrived at the cemetery was more suggestive of a spring day festivity. No one wore black, other than the odd pair of black trousers, and although there were tears, which was only natural, there seemed to be more smiles about. On top of all that, the sun shone brightly on the people and the cemetery.

The only people attending the funeral were the 'group', which consisted of Fred and Patrick, both supporting a much drained Peter, Don and Paul, Brad along with Simon and Derek, and a rather rotund Rabbi to conduct the service.

The entourage followed the coffin to the open grave and then halted, until the coffin had been lowered into the ground, at which stage they were then beckoned to come closer. They stood at what would be the base of the grave, huddled together with the sun blazing down on them. The Rabbi spoke first in Hebrew, which none of the 'group' understood, then he broke into English, so they then had a fair understanding of what was happening. The grave diggers, a couple of elderly men, stood a little way from the 'group' and they both wore hats while the rest of the attendees wore yarmulkes that had been handed to them at the entrance to the cemetery. Once the service was over, each friend of Keith's was invited to take up a spade from a grave digger and begin shoveling soil into the grave and onto the coffin. Once they had done a bit of filling in of soil, they were then required to plant the spade in the ground for the next person to pick it up and continue the task. Once each friend had done his bit of shoveling, the Rabbi said a prayer and it was over.

The men returned to the entrance to the cemetery, where they returned the borrowed yarmulkes and washed their hands before setting off to Fred's house to have a wake, while the grave diggers completed their task of filling in the grave with the remainder of the soil.

— — — — —

Back at Fred's house, they gathered out in the sunshine of the garden facing the sea, comforting each other and Peter in particular.

"I think you've been incredibly brave, Peter," commented Don, putting an arm around Peter's shoulder.

"I think it's more like the medication that's helped me along," answered Peter, solemnly.

"Well, whatever it is, I think you're coping well, Kid," continued Don.

Fred and Patrick had, in the meantime, busied themselves in the kitchen getting beers and soft drinks and then carrying them outside to the 'group'.

"Drinks are here guys. I'm sorry but I only have beers and soft drinks, so please help yourselves and let's drink a toast to Keith," said Fred, placing the tray with all the drink on a table.

"Just as a matter of interest," added Brad, "Do Jews have wakes after funerals?"

"Haven't a clue," responded Derek, "but if not, I'm sure that Keith would appreciate our gesture. Here's to Keith," said Derek, raising his beer bottle, as Fred had forgotten to bring the drinking glasses from the kitchen.

Everyone echoed Keith's name and they all drank a toast to him. Peter had remained stoic throughout the burial and it was only as they toasted Keith, that tears began to well up in his eyes, but no one commented on it and soon he had his emotions under control once more.

After the toast, the 'group' tended to split into smaller groups as people started to chat about everyday things. Some spoke of Keith and the things that he had done; little anecdotes coming to the fore, while others spoke of how life must just go on. It was during this period that Fred took Patrick to one side and got into animated discussion with him. This lasted for some time and then the two men rejoined the rest of the 'group'.

It was interesting to note that young Simon was more interested in chatting to the older men than the 'youngsters'. He stayed close to his Dad and Don, who were deep in conversation, while Paul remained his usual quiet self in the background. It was during one of these moments when Don and Derek were deep in conversation and Paul appeared to be left out of the conversation that Brad went and started chatting to him. This was not odd in any way as Brad was Paul's boss.

"Paul, sorry to talk shop here, but I was wondering how you were getting on working with Don?"

"Sorry Brad, but I don't understand."

"Are you happy in what you're doing?"

"Yes, very, thanks. Why do you ask?"

"I was just wondering if you had ever thought of coming to work at head office with me, selling property."

"To be perfectly honest, that had never entered my mind. You see, I get on very well with Don and I enjoy the outdoors. I don't think I'm and office-bound sort of person, Brad, but thank you for the consideration."

"Well any time you get bored and want a move, let me know."

"What are you two so deep in conversation about," interjected Don, who had finished talking to Derek and now focused his attention on Paul.

"Um, Brad was asking if I would like a job at head office," replied Paul, rather sheepishly, not knowing why Brad had offered it in the first place and not knowing how Don might take the offer.

"Do you want to work at head office?" queried Don.

"No, I told him that I was perfectly happy working with you and I preferred the outdoor to sitting behind a desk all day."

"Baby, I'll never stand in your way if you want to go and work there, or anywhere else for that matter. All I would say is think before you make any choices and sleep on it and see what tomorrow brings, but I won't stand in your way."

"You know how I feel about you. I'm happy working with you and happy spending my life with you, so I don't want to change anything," replied Paul, taking Don's hand in his and giving it a squeeze.

"You know how much I love you, Baby, and that is why I want you to think before you commit to anything that might affect your life and future."

Fred and Patrick approached Derek who had been making small talk to Simon.

"Derek, we'd like to have a word with you if you have a moment," said Patrick. "Fred and I have been wanting to take a holiday together at some stage…"

"… and you want me to look after the house for you?"

"No, not at all. In fact we have discussed this and we both agree that we'd like you to come on holiday with us."

Derek gave a small chuckle and then added, "That's extremely kind of both of you, but you know what they say 'two's company and three's a crowd'. I'm sure you would prefer to have some quality time alone and get your relationship back together again."

"We hear what you say, Derek, but I think that Patrick and I have a strong enough relationship without having to get it back together. In fact, it was Patrick's idea to ask you, but that doesn't mean I don't want you there. Of course I do. We actually thought of going on a cruise for about a week. So, what do you think?"

Derek was a little taken aback by the offer, but he also knew that he could do with a holiday and Simon wasn't a baby that needed looking after, so he could leave him at home.

"I don't know what to say, Guys."

"Just say yes," beamed Patrick.

Derek thought a moment longer then agreed.

"Okay, I'll join you."

"There is, however, one small catch to this," said Fred rather coyly.

"I knew there had to be a catch," laughed Derek. "There's always a catch when I get something or win something."

By this time, everyone had stopped speaking and was listening in to the conversation between Derek and Fred and Patrick.

"The real reason we want you to accompany us on the cruise is so that you can be Fred's best man," said Patrick.

"Best Man!" Boomed Derek's voice, at which point everyone's ears pricked up.

"Yes, Derek. Patrick and I are going on the cruise and going to get married at the same time. We had looked into it and found that we could have a civil service, and of course we do need a witness, so would you agree to be my best man and our witness?"

"I'm truly flattered," replied Derek, a little dumbstruck.

"Just remember Derek, that when Dad was married to my Mum and he used to sneak out to see you, you were the best man in his life, so I think it's appropriate that you be his best man at his wedding," said Peter.

It was the first time that Peter had a broad smile on his face and shed no more tears. Then there was a cacophony of well wishes from the rest of the guys there. There were kisses all round and hugs aplenty

"Do you remember what I said to you when you left here after bringing us the bad news about Keith, Derek?" asked Patrick. "I said, 'tomorrow' and here is tomorrow, another day, a fresh, new day and with it has come joy and happiness."

"You're right. I do remember that and it has turned into something special for you guys," answered Derek.

"So, can Fred and I get another big hug and a kiss from our future best man?" asked Patrick.

As Derek hugged and kissed both men, the others joined in to create one big happy kissing, hugging 'group', united in love.

About the Author

Lew Bull is a South African living in Johannesburg and has been published in a number of short story anthologies as well as having had nine novels and two collections of his own short stories published by Nazca Plains. He has also written a play called "Stark Raving Naked".

He has recently retired after 29 years of being involved in education, during which time he was awarded a doctorate in education, made a Fellow of the London College of Music for Speech and Drama and a Licentiate from Trinity College, London. He and his partner are currently in their thirty-sixth year of being together and he still likes to travel and write erotica.

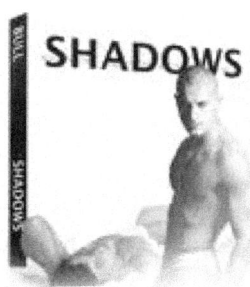

SHADOWS

A NOVEL BY
LEW BULL

The Bonds of

Lew Bull

A NOVEL BY
Lew Bull

and Willing

ROUGH CUT

LEW BULL

www.ingramcontent.com/pod-product-compliance
Lightning Source LLC
Chambersburg PA
CBHW051120260626
47170CB00005B/1592